SURGICAL Murders

BOOK 5

LAURA BURKE

Paperback: 978-1-963883-54-1
eBook: 978-1-963883-55-8
Library of Congress Control Number: 2024905638

Ordering Information:

Prime Seven Media
518 Landmann St.
Tomah City, WI 54660

Printed in the United States of America

CHAPTER 1

Jolene was glad to get back home. It had been a trying case. She was ready for a chance to sleep in and not have to get up early. Jolene's father was home as well. He didn't know about her injuries and was surprised when she walked through the door with her arm in a sling.

"What in the world happened to you?"

"Oh, it's nothing. I got shot with an arrow."

Her father was glad she was home. He couldn't imagine that Jolene was shot in the last case they were on, and this time, she was injured by an arrow. This was becoming a dangerous road she had chosen. But he had to respect her decision.

Although her injuries hadn't been fatal, he knew Agent Haines would protect her the best he could. She also had Agent Blay to protect her.

Jolene was genuinely committed to doing her part and using her abilities to solve these case files.

Jolene sat at the table amd was looking outside at the bird feeder. She had complained to her father the food kept getting wet when it rained. Now that spring was coming around the same problem would be happening. As she looked out she saw her father had made the roof of the feeder larger so now the food wouldn't become wet. She had to start laughing at.

The Director of the FBI wanted to give her an award for her services and the ability to close these cases and bring the guilty to justice. This gave the families the closure they had waited for.

The Director gave Jolene and Agent Haines, Blay, a couple of weeks to rest and recoup from her and Blay's injury. Even though it wasn't severe for Jolene, Agent Blay needed the time off. This also gave him the time to get to know Jolene better.

Agent Haines told Jolene that when she was ready, the Director asked him to take her to the storage facility and let her pick the next case she wanted to work on.

Agent Haines wanted to tell her but knew she'd want to go there the same day he told her. So, he kept it a secret. He did, however, tell her father and hoped he would keep the secret from Jolene. He had the most respect for Jolenes father.

Chief was so proud of Jolene that he was bursting his buttons off his shirt. He also had a severe worrying problem about Agent Blay and Jolene becoming too close. Would this affect the working relationship they had?

Agent Blay wanted to be close to Jolene, so he found an apartment in town where Jolene lived so he could be close to her. His love for her had grown, and he hoped her love for him was the same.

Agent Blay knew what the Director had said but didn't tell her. He told her he was on leave because of his injury. The apartment he rented was a two bedroom and small. He hadn't told Jolene, but he thought being close to Jolene would cut down on the travel time from the city. Agent Haines could stay with him when they were on a case.

Two weeks passed, and Jolene was getting fidgety. She wanted to get back to work. It was nice being off for a couple of days, but now it was time to get back out there in her mind.

Jolene sat by the window, just staring out into the garden. The flowers in full bloom. Then end of summer would fast approach. She knew winter would bring snow and cold weather to her area. The only thing Jolene wanted was to go back to work. She thought about calling Agent Haines, but thought she better not. He would be around when he had something to share.

"Dad, why can't they just care and assign a fresh case to us? This sitting around is making me crazy."

"Jolene, you know how serious Agent Blay, Elliot's wound was, so they just want to make sure he's able to go back to work. Do you want them to assign another agent to you and Agent Haines?"

"No, we three are like the three musketeers. We work well together and we know how each other thinks. It would be difficult to train another agent for us. We work together. Another Agent would just slow us down."

"So, wouldn't it be better to wait until Elliot's ready to go back out there?"

"Yes, I know, but at least Agent Haines and I could go over three more files in the meantime."

"No, the Director said there would be no work for a few weeks. He said all three of you need a break."

Agent Blay didn't mind the time off. It gave him more time to spend with Jolene on a personal level. His feelings grew more profound with each day. Now that he had moved to Parish, he didn't have to drive for four hours to see her. She kind of liked the idea he lived so close to her. He tried to keep his distance from her at first, but it was very hard.

Finally, Agent Haines and Agent Blay came over to Jolene's, and she knew it was to tell her they were returning to work. Boy, was she surprised when she opened the door.

Chief stood by his daughter's side and told the agents to come in. "Well, we have news from the Director. He is throwing a particular party for Jolene, and both of you are to attend."

"Oh, my." Jolene said.

"He's really proud of the progress we have made with the three cases we've solved. He also wanted to give you an award for being so diligent in how quickly you have come up with the closing of each."

"An award? I was just doing what we set out to do! Solve the case and give the families closure. I don't need an award. You two need to get the reward, not me."

"But look how long these cases have sat in that basement? With your ability and perseverance. We could solve these cases when no one else could."

"By the way, I was told it was a black tie affair so Chief I hope you have a tux. Jolene, I'll be your escort to the dinner, that is if you don't mind?" Agent Blay braded.

"You are sure it's black tie? I have one, but not sure if it still fits." Chief announced.

Jolene was overwhelmed; the Director had such powerful feelings for them. They were just doing what they knew best. Solving crime and putting away the bad guys.

The dinner was in an enormous hall, and when Jolene and her father walked in, her mouth dropped. There had to be at least fifty agents from the FBI there. She hadn't expected this, nor did her father.

Agent Haines escorted them to their table up to the front of the room. After they were seated, a waiter came over with a bottle of champagne and popped the cork.

The Director was up on a stage and giving a speech. The speech was about how the three of them had solved three cases in just a few weeks. He made it sound like the three of them were superstars. It made Jolene blush. Her face turning red with embarrassment. Her father beamed with a glow of proudness.

"Jolene, please come up here."

She proceeded to the platform and stood beside the Director. Not knowing what he was about to do made her even more nervous.

"Agent Jolene Johnson, on behalf of the Agency, we want to give upon you this plaque for a job well done."

"I didn't do it all by myself. I had two amazing partners." Jolene had tears running down her face.

The entire room stood up and applauded. Even Jolene's father was moved to tears.

"Now, that's the dedication I like to see in all my agents." The Director shook his finger at the other agents in the room and then laughed.

The waiters started bring out the food and everyone began eating. Most of the tables were making small talk between themselves. After their meal was done, a few of the Agents came up to Jolene and her partners to shake their hands. It would be a night to remember for sure.

The Director came up to Agent Haines shook his hand. "Did you tell Jolene what the other surprise is?"

"No, I was going to wait until tomorrow. Knowing Jolene like I do, well, she'd want to go there tonight."

"What are you guys talking about?" She asked.

"Well, I was going to wait until tomorrow. Boy, the Director is as bad as you."

"So, tell me what it is?"

CHAPTER 2

"Okay, I'll tell you. The Director said you are to pick out your own cases from now on. I'm taking you to the storage room and you are going to go through the files to see what we're going to work on."

"You're kidding, right? I get to see the room where these files are being kept?"

"Yes, you will see what we have down there and you are to go through the boxes to pick out the cases you think we need to work."

Jolene was excited to see this cellar they finally talked about. She did not know how overwhelming it would be. Agent Haines escort Jolene and her father to the hotel they had arranged for them to spend the night. Another Agent would see the Chief home in the morning.

The four-hour trip would be well worth the trip. This way he could get a few questions answered about Jolene. All the agents had questions about Jolene but knew not to ask Agent Haines or Agent Blay.

The following day, Agent Haines and Blay came knocking on the door of the chief's room. Chief Johnson was up, but Jolene was still sleeping. She wasn't used to drinking. The celebration was overwhelming, and she came to the hotel and had difficulty sleeping. She wanted to see the cellar they all talked about.

Chief Johnson knocked on her door to wake her up. There was no response. He opened the door to look in. Jolene, he called out softly. She started to stir.

"Hey girl, it's time to get up. Your playmates are here."

She jumped up and threw on her robe. Walking out to a sitting room, she saw both agents sitting there.

"Good morning!" Agent Haines spoke.

"Morning." She replied.

"Yes, but I want to get a shower first."

"You look fine." Agent Blay spoke up.

"Sure, I do! Can you imagine the guys down at the bureau if I walked in with my pj's on?"

"No, but I guess it would make their mouths drop!" Agent Haines replied.

"Well, I will not give them a chance to see me in my pj's!"

"I should hope not!" Chief Johnson put his two cents in.

Jolene showered and dressed for the day. She didn't wear makeup, so it didn't take her long to dress and was ready to go.

"Now, Jolene, please take your time and not overthink the cases you read. I'm sure you will be overwhelmed, and you have to remember these are all old cases, and you can't solve all of them at once." Her father was concerned.

"Oh, dad, you know I'll be extra careful with the case I choose."

"Chief, I'll make sure she stays with the program." Agent Haines spoke up. "After we have some breakfast, Agent Turk is going to escort, you home. Jolene is going to stay here and we'll bring her home after she has picked out our next case. You know she will want to use her blackboard to start the case."

"Yes, I know and if she could put it on her back, she would!" Chief Johnson stated.

"Okay, let's go." Jolene was in a hurry now that she was ready. "Do we have to eat breakfast can't we go to the cellar first? I'm sure I can pick out a case and then we can eat breakfast, how does that sound?"

"Boy, she's a pushy broad!" Agent Blay said. "We have to eat first!"

"Yes, she can be just that!" the chief agreed.

It took them about thirty minutes to arrive at the storage basement after they ate. The sun was shining. In Jolenes eyes it was a perfect day. Jolene was excited and couldn't wait to see what was in this secret room.

Agent Haines, drove over to the main office of the FBI. It took about twenty minutes. Jolene hadn't been to that office yet. The building was enormous. Larger that she had imagined. This in itself was a treat for her.

Look way up there. The Director's office is up there and you never want to be called to his office. So just remember that." Agent Haines teased her.

"Now Jolene, I should blindfold you until we get down there." Agent Haines told her.

"Oh, come on, it can't be that bad!"

"Jolene, you can't imagine!" Agent Blay spoke up.

"Come on guys, you're pulling my leg. Jolene, well, if you could see down in the ground, that's how far the building goes down. So remember the building you are entering goes down as far as it goes up."

They rode the elevator down to the cellar. When the doors opened, Jolene's mouth dropped. She became a little dizzy. The excitement and the ride in the elevator were overwhelming.

"You're kidding. These are cold cases?"

"Yes, from all over the United States. In 2019, there were nearly 17,000 cold cases."

"They are here?"

"Yes, that's why the Director has ordered us to clean up these cases. But not all at the same time." Agent Haines told her.

"I can't believe there are that many!"

The room was filled with boxes from the floor to the ceiling. All boxes are dated with the years of the cases inside. Jolene looked around and touched all the boxes she could reach.

"Jolene, these three boxes are the ones we're working from right now. So, look through these files first. If nothing appeals to you, we can pull down other boxes."

"No, if these are the ones we've been working on, we can continue with them. Since we started with them, we might clean them up before bringing down another box. That's fine. Let me look at the cases in those and see if something jumps out at me. It's not like we're going to be out of cases." Jolene announced.

That made Agent Haines and Blay to laugh.

"We'll be old and gray before we get even a half of these done!" Jolene said to Agent Haines.

"Well, let's get started." Jolene started pulling files out.

"Jolene, take the ones you think are suitable candidates for us. Put them in a pile here at the end of the table. Leave the ones you don't want right now in the box." Agent Haines told her.

Agent Blay couldn't help himself. He had to get in there with her. He was just as eager as Jolene.

"Let's see, we've solved three cases. Gunshot, smothering, stabbing, bow and arrow. So, what is left?" Jolene asked.

"We've covered everything but drowning."

"So, does that mean you want to find a case involving cases of drowning victims?" Blay asked.

"No, not really! But if we see one or two in these three boxes, we can look at the file."

"Okay, Elliot Blay, get your hands out of the box I'm looking at!" Jolene scolded.

"I'm just trying to help!"

"Yeah, I know. But you are messing up what I was doing. Also, you are stirring up the dust!"

"Oh, I see what you are talking about." He sneezed.

"Jolene, take it easy on the kid," Agent Haines said.

They all laughed. "If only the Director could see us now!"

Jolene had five case files she had pulled. They were in three different cities, but they all had the same M.O. She had carefully placed them at the end of the table.

Agent Haines picked them up and walked over to a small desk. He opened them one by one and read over the file. They were all in New York.

"Jolene, these cases are here in New York. Did you realize that?"

"No, sir. They all looked good. The one I had on top is the one I think we'll go with. What do you think?"

"The other two are interesting as well. They take place in West Virginia and Virginia. I'll leave them in the order you had them in, so if you change your mind, they will be right here."

"Okay, you know me so well. I will start dissecting the file before we leave."

"Is anyone else hungry around here? Blay asked.

Agent Haines and Jolene looked at their watches. It was two thirty in the afternoon. No wonder he was screaming for food!

"It's time to feed the animals!" Jolene spoke up.

"Jolene, do you want to break for lunch?" Agent Haines asked.

"Yes, I suppose it would be a good idea. That way I can think better if we walk away for a half hour."

"There is a pizza store just down the block we can walk to and the pizza is out of this world! The sauce is so thick, and if you add pepperoni, peppers, mushrooms, it's so thick you can't hardly get your mouth on it!"

"Okay, I guess we're going for pizza." Agent Haines stated.

"But what if I want a hamburger?" Jolene asked, teasing him.

"Come on Jolene. You love pizza as much as I do." He said in a pleading voice.

Jolene was laughing at him, and Agent Haines knew she was kidding. They headed for the elevator.

They reached the outside, and the sunlight was so bright Jolene had to shield her eyes. She hadn't realized how dark it was in the cellar, even with the lights on.

"Jolene, are you okay?" Agent Haines asked.

"Yes, it was just a shock when you walk out and the sunlight hits, ya."

"Yeah, and it takes a few minutes for your eyes to adjust."

"Maybe you should bring your sunglasses tomorrow." Agent Haines suggested.

"Yes, that would be a great idea. Too bad we're so far away from my house. I could have dad bring them to me." Jolene answered.

"You picked out three files. Are they the ones you want to start on?" Agent Haines asked.

"Well, I'm not sure yet. I have to inspect each of them and then decided. You know this is like when you bring the three to the house. I have to go over them each and see which one I think needs to be settled first." Jolene answered.

"I know you will be careful in your consideration. I'm not pushing you. You know there are plenty of cases to look at." Agent Haines told her.

Agent Blay kept bugging Jolene to give him a clue about what she had put aside for them to work on. She just ignored him. This didn't sit well with him. He knew how she was. This differed from before. They picked out the three cases and let Jolene pick from them. Now the tables were turned. She got to pick out three cases and decided which one they would work.

This was an unfamiliar experience for him. Agent Haines and Agent Blay always picked out three files to take to Jolene. Now she had full access to the basement. He felt left out. He knew it wouldn't do him any good to pressure her or try to make her give up the three cases she was considering. She would just tell him to give her a break and she would decide.

Agent Haines looked at Blay and didn't want to say anything. He knew he'd get over it. The pizza was good and Jolene kept her time in eating. Agent Haines knew she was thinking about which case to decide. The sun was setting and not so bright now. After finishing, they headed back to the basement.

CHAPTER 3

Jolene pulled the file off the desk and told Agent Blay to come over to discuss the case. This put a smile on his face. Even Agent Haines put a smile on his face and pulled his chair closer to the table Jolene was working on.

"Okay Jolene, let's go over the case."

"I'm ready. Well, this case involves three murder victims in three towns. The first was in Troy, New York. The second was in Albany, New York, and the third was in Malta, New York."

Agent Haines looked over the file, and the photographs included in it. He laid them out on the table. As he read over the medical examiner's report.

It was apparent they were killed in the same manner. No drugs were found in any of the victims. The officers and the detectives working the cases had made a note these ladies were prostitutes. This was confirmed by one of the detectives, but there wasn't any evidence to that fact. There were no witnesses to the assaults. Plus, the three murder victims were killed in the same manner and there was no sexual assault noted in any of the victims but, the problem being the coroner didn't do a rape kit.

"The reason they were put in the cold case bins was they had no identification on them, and they seem to have been killed late in the night. Each was found in a local park, nude and with no identification."

"So, they didn't count in the eyes of the police working the cases." Jolene said in an angry voice.

Jolene, it was not; they just didn't have enough to go on. They asked questions, but nobody in the towns they were killed in seems to know them.

"Maybe they were brought to these towns by the killer. Not from the towns at all."

"Is there any mention of them reaching out to neighboring towns to see if anyone recognizes them?"

Agent Blay said, "they sent out photos to the neighboring towns and nobody appeared to know any of them."

"Yes, that could have been a possibility, but if they sent out photos of the women, somebody had to have known them."

"It doesn't appear they knew each other, either." Agent Haines bought up.

"They all look like they were in their twenties. The medical examiner agrees they were in their twenties."

"Do you think this could be someone they dated? I didn't see any rings on their fingers. There was no jewelry found on any of them, not even a necklace." Jolene stated.

"See, you're are so observant." Agent Haines told her.

"What did the medical examiner say was the instrument that killed them?" Blay asked.

"He said it appeared to be a sharp weapon, like a switchblade knife or something similar. He wasn't sure."

"He didn't try very hard."

He knew exactly what Jolene was thinking, and he knew if she pushed the issue, she would get her way. The bodies being busied for this long wouldn't really give them any evidence at this point.

"Jolene no! We can't dig them up. Besides, they have been buried for nearly five to eight years." Agent Haines knew her so well.

"I know! Look at the marks on both sides of their neck. The carotid arteries were slashed, not just one side, but both. Who would kill someone like that?"

"The examiner also states all three had their breast removed by another instrument."

"The police reports didn't mention that in their investigation. Were they nude or dressed? Did he check and do a rape kit on them?" Jolene was getting down to the bare facts.

"No, they didn't do a rape kit on any of them."

"So, I guess this is the case we're going to take on?" Agent Blay asked.

Agent Haines looked at Jolene. He could see in her expression she was all fired up and ready to hit the road. She had already made several notes and was ready to investigate this case. There were notes they were nude and had had none sexual indications. But where did their clothes go? Did the police check the local dumpsters? This wasn't in the file.

"Jolene, what do you want to do with these other two cases?" Agent Haines asked.

"We'll do them after we take care of this one. Is that alright?" Jolene stated.

"Sure, I'll leave them right here so we don't have to look through the box again. Besides, as you can see, there are plenty of cases for us to work. I'm sure there will be plenty for us to work. The Director wants us to clean up these files." Agent Haines announced.

"That means I'll be old and gray by the time we're halfway done! If we're lucky, that is."

"You mean we'll be great grandparents!" Blay announced.

Agent Haines began laughing at his statement. He had to think of something to say. "You mean if anyone will have you and you have children?"

Jolene laughed at that statement.

"Okay guys, this is serious. We need to concentrate. Let's go eat and then we can come back and dig in. Or, if you guys prefer, we can head to my hotel and tomorrow, my house and the black- board."

"We're going to have to get a blackboard down here!" Agent Haines announced.

"It might help, but we'd still have to go back to my house. Now that Blay has an apartment in town, you can always stay with him. This makes it perfect." Jolene stated.

"Yeah, and I can see what kind of housekeeper he is. Plus, see what groceries he keeps." Agent Haines stated.

"Well, let's stop all of this gabbing and go to dinner. We can take the file with us so we don't have to come back to this dusty basement!" Blay was eager to get to the restaurant.

Jolene put the files in her briefcase. She always carried it with her when she was working on a case. Agent Haines always kept a small travel bag in the car's trunk in case he was called out of town. Agent Blay consistently delayed packing until the ultimate moment. No matter how hard they tried to get him to be prepared, he always waited until the last minute.

"Okay, what's it going to be, pizza or fried chicken?" Jolene asked and looked straight at Agent Blay. She knew him so well. As they hit the street Jolene couldn't believe how hot it still was and it was eight thirty at night. Usually, it had started to cool down by now.

"What are you looking at me for?" He asked.

"Well, because it depends on what you feel like eating. You're the one that's hungry!" Jolene stated.

"Oh, so you're putting the blame on me!" He replied.

"I vote for chicken. We had pizza for lunch." Agent Haines told them.

"Okay, there is a chicken right across from the pizza place just down the street. They have pretty good chicken. I vote we go there. That way, we don't have to drive anywhere."

"Fine by me. Just so we can eat something!"

Agent Haines and Jolene began laughing. Agent Blay just stood there, looking at both of them. He wanted to say something to both of them, but decided to just keep his mouth shut.

After eating, they returned to the main building where Agent Haines had parked his car. They were off to Jolene's hotel. She looked at her watch and saw it was nearly nine o'clock. All of them were tired and just wanted to forget the day and sleep. Tomorrow would be another day. Agent Haines dropped Jolene off, and then Agent Blay.

Jolene was up at four in the morning. Her mind was on her blackboard, sitting in the dining room, ready for her. It even seemed to call out to her. She was in New York. She looked out at the city and all the lights from the tall office buildings. She couldn't imagine living in a place like this. Jolene thought about her home in Parish with a population of only around three thousand. Everyone knew everyone and they all said hello to each other. She thought it might be the fact her father was the chief of police and everyone knew him and their neighbors.

She was really surprised her father hadn't moved it into another room. He was always complaining about it being in the way. She knew He was kidding her, for he always bragged about her. Chief knew it was a hard job, but she was good at it. With Jolene working with the FBI, he was busting his buttons on his uniform from being so proud of her.

Agent Haines showed up at the Hotel around seven and knew Jolene would be awake and ready to go. He picked up the courtesy phone in the lobby and called her room.

"Good morning, Jolene, I'm in the lobby. Want to have some breakfast before we hit the road?"

"Sure, sounds good to me. Is Agent Blay with you?" She asked.

"No, I think he drove back to Parish last night. Anyway, it's just you and I this morning and on the road." Agent Haines commented.

"Sounds good to me. I wanted to talk to you about something, anyway. I hope you don't mind."

"Jolene, you can come to me anytime about anything. You don't have to worry, it's just between you and me, okay?"

"Great, I think you already know, Agent Blay, Elliot and I have been seeing each other and I really have feeling for him. I know the reason he took the apartment in my home town it was to be closer to me. But I know it will cut down on travel time from New York to my house."

"Jolene, I don't know if you know it or not, but Elliot came and talked to me about you and him. I told him the samething I'm going to tell you. Your personal business is yours and his. As long as it doesn't interfere with working a case and as long as you both do your job, I have no problem with it. But if it interferes with the job or you both become stupid, then I'll remove him from the case. Do you understand?" Agent Haines explained.

After breakfast, they picked up Jolene's luggage and Agent Haines loaded it in the truck of his car. The sun was up and glowing. The position of it was strong through the windshield. This would not be a fun ride home unless she could find some sunglasses.

"Agent Haines, can you stop at a Walmart or some type of drugstore?"

"Sure, I guess you need to pick up those sunglasses, huh?"

"You got it," Jolene said with a smile.

Agent Haines cell phone began ringing. He knew who it was before answering. "Hello Agent Blay."

"Are you two on your way? You know it's going on nearly ten o'clock and we have a lot to do!" Agent Blay asked.

"Yes, we're on our way. In fact, we are about an hour away. So, hold your horses. We'll be there before noon. Is that alright with you?" Agent Haines was trying to get under his skin.

Jolene pulled the file out of her briefcase and began going over it. Discussing it with Agent Haines made her go over questions she had. There was too much information missing from the file. Even Agent Haines questioned the reports and the reports from the police department's detectives.

At exactly twelve noon, they pulled into the driveway at Jolene's house. Jolene called Agent Blay and told him they were there to come over and bring lunch. Agent Haines laughed at her statement. Agent Blay was always complaining he was hungry and always ready to eat.

Jolene walked in and was surprised that her father had made some changes while she was gone. He had cleaned her board. Put new chalk laid out and two new erasers all in a row. Plus, he put a card out that told her he was proud of her and he loved her. He had drawn a big smiley face at the bottom. It brought tears to Jolene's eyes.

It didn't take long for Agent Blay to show up. He brought Chinese food. It was one of Jolene's favorite and Agent Haines liked it too.

"So, what did you two discuss on the ride home?" Agent Blay asked.

Jolene was feeling playful. "We discussed your haircut!"

"Come on Jolene, you know we talked about his shoes and how shiny they are. You could see you face in them!" Agent Haines commented.

Agent Blay hung his head. He didn't know what to say or come back with. He knew they were just kidding, but some how he took it seriously.

"Come on Blay, we didn't really talk about much of anything. Jolene was talking about how summer would be over and how the trees would change their colors. It seemed like the temperatures were still are up there. Thanks for asking."

CHAPTER 4

After they finished lunch, Jolene and Agent Haines cleaned the table and they got ready to start on the case. Jolene made three columns on the board. Labeling each for the victims. Jane Doe 1, Jane Doe 2, Jane Doe 3, then drawing a line between them. Taking the coroner's report, she wished she could call him and ask him some questions because of the time she didn't dare.

They had put nearly half the board information, including questions they needed answers to. Before they knew it, Chief Johnson came through the door.

"Hey you guys, don't you guys ever quit?" He asked.

"Yes, and we were just closing down for the night." Jolene answered.

Jolene's phone rang. It was seven in the morning. "Hello?"

"Good morning! I knew you would be up. Are you ready for company?"

"Sure, come on over. Are you at Blay's?"

"No, I went home. I'm on my way after I stop for donuts. I expect Elliot won't be far behind."

"You're right. If he smells donuts, he'll beat you here!" Jolene snickered.

"You got that right. I should be there in about fifteen. Is Chief up yet?" He asked.

"Yes, he's in the kitchen making coffee."

"Great!"

Fifteen minutes passed, and two vehicles pulled up in the driveway. Chief looked out and saw Haines and Blay getting out of their cars.

"Your boss is here and you boyfriend."

"Oh, Dad. Don't call him my boyfriend. We're working a case."

"Sorry. I'll let them in."

"Boy, that coffee smells wonderful. With these donuts, we're all set." Agent Blay announced.

Jolene got the cups from the cabinet. The sugar and cream. Chief put the donuts on a tray, and before anyone could get their hands on them, Blay had already picked up one.

"Boy, you don't wait for anyone!" Agent Haines told him.

"Well, you're the one who woke me up at six!"

"I bet Jolene has been up since four and you complain about being woken up at six? What a baby!" Haines and Chief both laughed.

"Son, you are going to learn fast you can't over sleep around Jolene. When she has something on her mind, she goes for the brass ring!" Chief explained to Blay.

"Brass ring, sir?"

"Oh, I forgot you are still a youngster. Back a long time ago, at the fair, the merry-go-round had a brass ring on a pole. When you rode around, you had to grab it. If you did, grab it. You would get ten or twenty rides on the merry-go-round for free. There was only one problem. It was always set just out of reach for anyone trying to grab it."

"You are kidding?"

Agent Haines spoke up. "Yes, and there were many of guys that would spend ten or more dollars trying. They wanted the extra rides for their girlfriends. This would prove to her how much he cared for her."

"Okay, can we get to the case, guys?"

"Sure."

"I've made three columns, one for each Jane Doe. Now we have to put under each where they were found and the date they were found."

"Jane Doe one was found in Troy, New York. They found her in a nearby park. The second and third were also found in nearby parks. The victims were approximately two to three days apart." Agent Haines spoke up.

"The medical examiner, Troy Cane, was called to each scene. His assistant took pictures of the victims and where they were found. They were moved to his office for him to finish examining them and to do an autopsy on all three." Agent Haines explained.

"After the first one came in, it was easy to look for similar points in the victims." Jolene stated.

"I wanted to call him this morning, but knew it was too early to call. Besides, I think we should see him in person."

"I agree. Talking with the coroner and being able to show him these photos will jog his memory."

"We can go today?" Agent Haines requested.

"Should we call him first?" Agent Blay asked.

"No, we shouldn't! He would just put us off. If we just show up, he'll have to see us." Jolene insisted.

"Alright, let's load up and take off." Agent Haines is in complete agreement with Jolene.

The drive to the coroner's office was only a short distance from Jolene's house, about thirty minutes.

When they arrived, the secretary asked if they had an appointment?"

When they told her no, she said he didn't have time to see them. They would have to make an appointment.

Jolene voiced, making the disappointment they felt because they were being put off.

"Look, we're from the FBI, and it is essential to see him now. So, whatever you have to do, do it now and get him out here."

"Doctor Cane, there are three agents from the FBI here to see you."

"Thank you Sofie, I'll be right out."

"Hello, I'm Dr. Cane. How can I help you?"

"Dr. Cane, were looking into the death of three women you were the medical examiner on."

"Do you have their names?"

"No sir, these women were never identified. Their bodies were found in local parks in Troy, Albany, and Malton. We have photos of the women, if that helps."

"Let's go to my office. Oh, I seem to remember something like that. They were killed like two or three days apart, right?"

"Yes, that's what you have in your notes." Jolene answered.

"That was a very unusual case. Let me see the photograph you have. I'll have to pull my files on them. We keep copies of all the reports we send in. I take it they were never solved? They still don't know who they were?" Dr. Cane exclaimed.

"Yes sir. The cases were sent to the cold case files. The detectives, in the cases, weren't able to find any information on the three women." Agent Haines spoke up.

"Ah, here we are. The women had rope burns on their wrists and ankles. That meant they were restrained. They also had bruising on their face, like someone had punched them."

"Would have the abuse killed them?"

"No, I don't believe so. But it would have knocked the woman unconscious. By doing so he or she would have been able to restrain them. There was chloroform in their toxicology, but no other drugs."

"Sir, were the women sexually assaulted?"

"That was not noted on any of the women. The only thing we found was the females were naked. All three were bound with the same type of rope, which was put in the forensic box."

"What about the incisions on the bodies?" Jolene was on a roll.

"The wounds were unusual. The incisions on the neck were precise, measuring one inch and a half over the jugular vein on both sides. But what I don't understand is what kind of weapon was used. The breast was obliterated, but both breasts were removed with a different instrument, one that cauterized the tissue as it removed them. The victims would have bled out from the wounds on the neck. There was no bleeding from the breast. The incision which removed the breast was also surgically sutured using a number two suture material."

"Would you say the person who did this had medical knowledge?"

"I really can't say. But it would appear they had some medical instruments to accomplish this. I mean, look, it would have been someone who had surgical experience at best." The doctor was shaking his head as he spoke.

"So, if I understand you correctly, this could have been a person who had some type of medical training and may have been a physician!"

"That isn't what I'm saying; you must draw your own conclusions." He became very nervous.

Agent Haines stepped in. "Thank you, Dr. Cane. If we have questions, we'll contact you?"

"You're welcome."

Agent Blay just stood there, not saying anything. He marveled in watching Jolene work.

They left, and Jolene continued making her notes. The blackboard would be packed once they arrived back at Jolene's house.

"Jolene, how about we order a pizza for dinner? I have a feeling this is going to be a long night." Agent Haines asked.

"If we call them now, it will be there by the time we arrive. Dad will be there if it comes before we arrive. Let's order two." Jolene said.

"Sounds good to me." Agent Blay spoke up.

They pulled into the driveway just as the pizza delivery person pulled up. The chief must have seen him, for he had the front door opened, waiting for him.

"Great, I was wondering what to have for dinner. Thanks, guys." He commented.

"Hey, dad I don't think so!" Jolene remarked.

Jolene started adding her notes to the board. Just as Agent Haines said, the board was filling up fast. They still had to speak to the detectives on the cases. That would be tomorrow.

"Jolene, what are we doing tomorrow?" Agent Haines asked.

"Well, tomorrow, we must see the detectives who worked these cases. They could remember something they forgot to put in the report. I doubt it, but it will be worth a try."

"Yes, but the cases are so old, they probably have forgotten everything about them." Agent Blay stated.

"This case was so unusual they might remember something. Anyway, it's worth a try."

"Look, you guys have been there before. It always works out. You must have faith it'll work out again." Chief replied and smiled at Jolene.

"Yes, dad is right. We've been there before. We'll sort this out and we'll solve this case as well." Jolene said with confidence.

"I'll call it a night. Blay and I are going to retire for the night. We'll pick you up, Jolene, at about seven. Is that okay?"

"Yes, that will be fine. I'll be ready."

"Yea, you know Jolene will be ready!" Agent Blay complained.

"Look, we want to get to the first detective when he arrives. That way, he won't be tied up." Jolene replied.

CHAPTER 5

Jolene was up at four. She wanted to make her notes to ask the detectives. She hoped they would remember the cases. Only two detectives worked on these cases, so they should remember them.

Before she was through, she had two sheets of questions outlined to ask them. All were important and would help her determine if the bodies had been dumped in these parks after death. Jolene was pretty sure they had. The question on her mind was, what town did they come from?

Jolene was dressed and ready to ride. At seven-fifteen, she heard the car pull up in the driveway. Chief had just gotten up.

"Bye dad, see you tonight, or I'll call to let you know we're not coming home."

"Be safe Jolene. No gun shots, no arrows in the shoulder." He kissed her on the cheek.

She returned the kiss and was out the door. It was a brisk morning, and a jacket was required, but the temperature was supposed to go up in the eighties.

As she got into the car, she began giving orders to Agent Haines.

"We're going to Troy first and Albany second. From what the report stated, the detective in Albany handled the case in Malta."

"Okay, we're off. Do you have your questions ready Jolene?" Agent Blay asked.

Agent Haines laughed. "When has Jolene ever not been ready?"

"Yeah, I know, but I thought maybe she might want to run things by us before we get there." Agent Blay said.

"No, there isn't anything I need to run by you. Just jump in where you want once we start."

"Okay." Agent Blay replied.

It was a good forty-five-minute drive to the police station. Jolene was in the back seat going over her questions. She was ready and looking to drill the detectives on these cases!

They walked into the police station and asked to see Detective Hindes. The desk sergeant asked if they had an appointment. This annoyed Jolene.

"Does everybody have to make an appointment these days to get anything done!" Jolene started raising her voice.

"No, we don't have an appointment. We're from the FBI and want to speak to the detective in charge of a murder case he investigated." Agent Haines spoke up.

"Oh, I'll tell him you're here. One minute please." He picked up the telephone and dialed his extension.

"Hello, Detective Hindes, there are three FBI agents here that want to see you. Should I send them back?"

"Yes, send them back."

He stood up and shook their hands as they approached his desk.

"Hello, what can I do for the FBI?" He asked.

"I'm Agent Johnson, this is Agent Haines, and Agent Blay. We want to ask you about a cold case you worked a few years ago."

"Oh? What case was that?"

"It involved a woman found in your park."

"I don't seem to remember a case like that."

"Let me give you some facts about the case. It might jog your memory." Agent Haines stepped in.

"It was a young woman, nude, cuts on both sides of her neck, both her breast had been removed and she was tied up."

"Oh yeah," I remember that case. We sent it to the FBI, for we had no suspects nor the identity of the victim."

Jolene took over from there. "Was the area sweep for clues to her identity?"

"Look, we're a small town, and everyone here knows everyone. We went around the neighborhood and asked if anyone knew her, and they all said the same thing. They had never seen her before."

"Did you ask the local bars if they had seen her that evening of her death?"

"Yes, we have two bars in town and we went to both. Neither of the bartenders or waitress had seen her before."

"What about the park, did your forensic team go over the area of the park and beyond to see if there were signs of blood or anything that might have fallen off the victim?" Jolene was putting on the pressure.

"Look, we're a small town, like I said. We had to call a forensic team from Albany to work the crime scene. They found nothing. Not even a drop of blood."

"So, in your opinion the body had been dumped in your park after death?"

"That was the conclusion of the forensic team. They said with the type of lacertians there should have been at least a drop of blood found if she had of been killed here."

"Thank you for your time, Detective." Jolene was ready to move on. She started for the door. Agent Haines and Blay trailed behind her.

Jolene turned, "Detective one last question. "Did you notice the restrains on the body?"

"Restraints? No, I didn't see any that I can remember. At least my notes, doesn't have it in the file."

"What about the clothing, did you check the dumpsters in the area to see if maybe her clothes had been dumped in a dumpster?" Jolene started raising her voice.

"Look we covered the area the best we could." He hollered back. "We found nothing!"

"Thank you, Detective." Jolene snapped back. Jolene turned and walked out with Agent Haines and Blay.

They got in the car, and Jolene looked puzzled.

Agent Haines saw the look on her face. "Jolene what's the matter?" He asked.

"I have a problem. If the women were nude, their clothes had to be somewhere close to where they were killed, or did he remove their clothes at the scene where he left the bodies?"

"And?" Agent Blay asked.

"They said they combed the area well. Was that just the park or did they check the dumpsters nearby?"

"Oh, I see what you're talking about. The detective nor Dr. Cane didn't say a word about any clothing being found." Agent Haines remarked.

"Maybe we'll have better luck with the forensics team finding something they didn't put in the file." Jolene was deep in thought. "Maybe the Detective in Albany we'll have better luck with."

"We'll be there in about five minutes. Do you want to speak to the detective first or the forensics captain first?" Agent Haines asked.

"Let's speak to the detective first and then the forensics captain."

"Okay with me. Whatever you want."

"Look this time we'll pull our badges out before we speak." Jolene stated.

They pulled into the parking lot of the police station. They walked in and up to the desk sergeant. He looked at them like they were criminals!

All three of them pulled out their badges and waved them at him. He immediately sat up straight and put a smile on his face.

"What can I do for you Agents?" He asked with a smile on his face.

"We would like to speak to Detective Joe Hudson." Jolene said with a smile on her face.

"I'll check and see if he's here. I know he went out on a call a little while ago. I don't know if he's back or not." He picked up the phone and dialed his extension.

After three rings, they heard him holler out. "Yes, what do you want?"

"Sir, there are three FBI agents here to see you."

"What the hell do they want?" He barked back. He didn't know they were within earshot of the conversation.

"Sir, I don't know. Should I send them back?"

"Yes, send them on back. I don't know why the FBI would be here! I don't have time for this."

"He said to go on back. Sorry about his tone. He's had a rough week!"

"That's okay, we're used to being greeted that way." Jolene told him with a smile.

They walked through the double doors and found his desk. It was piled high with files, and some were on the floor. It looked like he had more than he chose to deal with.

Jolene jumped in with both feet. She wanted him to know she wasn't scared of his bark!

"Detective Hudson, I'm Agent Johnson, this is Agent Haines, and Agent Blay. We would like to ask you a few questions about a case you worked few years ago."

"Yeah so? I've worked several cases. What case are you talking about?" He barked back.

"The case we're referring to involved two women you investigated from your town and in Malta. We understand you handled both cases." Jolene barked right back.

"So, I handle several cases. Which one are you talking about?" He asked in a mellow tone.

"It involved two women killed and dumped in your park and in Malta park. They were nude, bound with rope and their jugular vein cut on both sides." Jolene left off about their breast.

"Oh, you're talking about the women who had their breast removed also, right?"

"So, you do remember the case." Agent Haines spoke up.

"Yes, the darndest thing I've ever seen. It was rather cold that night to. I remember when this person called the station and told us he had found a body in the park. It was dark out and he just happened to stumbled over this body."

"Did you get the good guy's name who called it in?"

"No, and when I arrived, he was gone. A crowd gathered, and if he was in the crowd, he didn't show he knew anything about it."

"Did you and the forensic team go over the area well?"

"We did and we asked the locals in the area if they heard anything or saw anything suspicious. Nobody heard or saw anything. The park was usually used as a meeting place for couples. We thought maybe this was one of those times when the husband caught his wife cheating on him."

"You have a lot of that here?" Jolene asked.

"No, I just meant, sometimes two people meet in the park after dark and talk."

"Oh, I know what you meant." Jolene knew what he meant, and she wasn't accepting his excuse.

"What about the one in Malta, the same results found there?"

"It was precisely the same. It was a mirror of the case here. I heard there was also one found in Troy. Is that true?"

"Yes, exactly the same. Someone must have known these ladies."

"So why is the FBI involved with these cases."

That was the wrong thing to ask!

"Look, these women were someone. They have families who don't know what happened to their love one. They could have been married, had children. They were in the wrong place and ended up dead with nobody accountable. We're going to find the SOB who did this and give them closure. That's what we're doing investigating this case!" Jolene gave it to him with both barrels.

Agent Haines could see the smoke coming from Jolene's ears! He knew he had to get her out of there before she really let him have it.

"Detective, who is the captain over at the forensic office?" Agent Haines asked.

"That would be Captain Lowe. Do you want me to call over there and let him know you're coming over to see him?"

"No that won't be necessary!" Jolene barked back at him.

"Thank you, Detective Hudson." Agent Haines said as he shook his hand.

Jolene was out the door, and Agent Blay was right beside her.

"Jolene, you have to control yourself. He was definitely over worked and having a bad day. It wasn't anything against us. You were a little hard on him."

"Oh yeah? Do you think I was hard on him? Let me tell you something! These detectives could care less about these women! But if it were their family, they would pull out all the stops to solve it. No, I wasn't hard on him! I gave him something to think about!"

Agent Haines walked up behind them and heard Jolene giving Agent Blay a piece of her mind.

"Jolene, is everything alright? We can take a break. I know you were upset by his attitude but, remember we deal with this type all the time."

"Yes, I know. But it's like they don't even care! That's what I hate the most. It's as if nobody cares Agent Haines."

"Yes, I know, but remember, we're there and we care. We'll get to the bottom and catch the perp who did this. Remember that."

"Yeah Jolene, that's what we do. You're the best and we'll get the guy just remember we care." Agent Blay told her and gave her a hug.

"I know guys. Thank you for being there for me."

"Always." Agent Haines said.

"Let's go and have some lunch and then go see Captain, what was his name?"

Jolene started laughing. "You must be starving; your brain isn't working! Captain Lowe Agent Blay."

"Yes, I think we'll have lunch than see Captain Lowe." Agent Haines announced.

They found a quiet-looking cafe just three blocks away. It was noon, and the place was packed. A couple of factories were in the area, and it looked like all the employees came there to eat lunch. They walked in and were greeted by a little old lady.

"Sorry, but it'll be a few minutes before I have a table open. Please, do you mine waiting a few minutes."

"No problem, we'll wait."

Jolene brought her notebook in and began making notes on their discussion with the detective. She knew she had been overly bearing with him, but her thoughts aligned with her feelings. Agent Haines and his boss knew Jolene was the right person for the job. She always got results and closed the cases.

"Jolene, now when we see Captain Lowe you have to promise me you will be gentler with him." Agent Haines told her.

"Okay, I promise. But if he starts first, I can't guarantee anything."

They all three started to laugh. The little old lady came over and told them she had a table open if they wanted it.

They stood up and followed her to the table. Once seated, she asked them what they would like to drink. She gave them the menu and left to get their drinks.

Agent Blay looked over the menu and decided right away what he wanted. Jolene wasn't in the mood to eat, but there was soup on the menu, so she ordered it. Agent Haines decided he'd have the hamburger and fries.

"You guys have no idea as to how much fat is in these meals. Think about your cholesterol!" Jolene was shaking her head in disapproval.

"Hey, it's our cholesterol!" Agent Blay spoke up.

It only took a few minutes for their food to come out. "Young lady, are you sure you don't want something else besides soup?" She asked in a concerned voice.

"No ma'am, soup is all I want, thank you for your concern." Jolene responded.

"Okay but if you change your mind, just let me know."

"See that's what I'm talking about! People care about one another. The waitress doesn't even know me or us and yet she is still concerned about me."

"Yes, Jolene not everyone is the same. You know that." Agent Blay spoke up.

"Yes, I know. But isn't in nice to see someone that does care?"

They ate their lunch in silence.

"After lunch, let's take a ride over to the park where the second victim was found." Jolene asked.

"We could do that if you want." Agent Haines agreed.

Agent Haines paid the bill, and they were off to the park. He didn't know what she was looking for, but she must have a reason for wanting to go there.

Once they were at the park, she looked around.

CHAPTER 6

An elderly man was sitting by himself on a bench. He looked like he had lost his best friend. It was normal for Jolene to notice people who looked sad or happy. This guy was definitely sad. Jolene walked up to him and said hello. She hoped she could cheer him up.

He replied hello back to her. He now had a smile on his face.

"My name is Jolene. May I ask you a couple of questions?" She asked.

"My name is Joe. Sure, it's not every day I have a pretty young thing ask me questions."

"Thank you, sir for the compliment."

"What do you want to know?"

"Do you live here in the area?" Jolene spoke softly. Agent Haines and Agent Blay stood back and listened.

"Yes, I've lived here all of my life. See that house over there? That was where I was born, and that's where I'll die."

"Then you must know many things that go on around here."

"Yes, I do. Sometimes I know more than I care to remember."

"Do you know what goes on around here in the park?"

"Sometimes, why?"

"Do you remember about a woman who was found here in the park few years ago?"

"That was a naked woman, right?"

"Yes, she had been murdered. Did the police ask you if you saw anything suspicious that night?"

"No, they didn't even come to my door. They all know me around here. I thought it rather funny they didn't ask if I saw anything; they put up that yellow tape around the area, and as soon as the police took her body away, they took the tape down."

"Did you see someone put her body in the park?"

"I saw a car drive over the curb and take something out of the trunk. But I don't remember the type of car it was."

"In the lights on the street, did you see the person who took her body from the trunk?"

"I thought it was a man. But it's been so long ago I don't remember much of the details.

"Did you call the police about the body?"

"Yes, but I didn't give them my name. I thought it best. They would have thought I was just a meddling old fool."

"Why would they have thought that of you?"

"Well, you see, anytime anything happens in our neighborhood, I'm like the town watch. I always report things to the police. That night I thought it best to keep my identity to myself or they wouldn't have come out."

"I see, but you did report it, and the police did respond."

"Yes, and that detective came to."

"You mean Detective Hudson came out to?"

"Yeah."

"You sound like you don't think much of him. Have you had a run in with him?"

"You could call it a run in. I called him when a bunch of punks were spray painting the trees in the park and he told me to mind my own business!"

"I gather nothing was done to stop them. Am I right?"

"Look around you see all the trees that have been spray painted? Now they are defacing the building around here. They have done several houses on our block and they even have broken windows. Does the police care? Hell, no they just laugh it off and tell us to move if we don't like the neighborhood."

"Here is my card Joe, if you think about anything else about that night will you give me a call?"

"Sure, I like talking with you." He shook her hand.

"Thank you for talking to me. I'd like to introduce my two partners. This is Agent Haines and Agent Blay. They work with me. I'm so glad I got to meet you."

They shook his hand and told him if he needed anything to call Jolene and she'd see to it they got it done.

Joe smiled widely and told them he was glad he got to know Jolene and he'd treasure her card. Agent Haines and Blay gave him their cards also.

They walked away and Jolene looked back at Joe. He looked so lonely sitting there by himself. She gave a wave of her hand to him and he waved back with a big smile on his face.

Once they were in the car, Jolene made notes in her book.

"Okay now let's go and see Captain Lowe."

"You got it lady."

As they headed for the car, Jolene smiled ear to ear. Agent Blay looked at her as if she had swallowed a canary. Even Agent Haines noticed. They both wondered what she had on her mind.

"Jolene, what in the world?" Agent Haines asked.

"You heard Joe. See he had information that was never in the report. This is what I was looking for."

"You got all that from Joe, right?" Agent Blay asked.

"Yes, they didn't go to the neighbors at all. Besides that, they took down the crime scene tape before the forensic team basically arrived to go over the area."

"Oh, I see. Yes, you are right. The Detective Hudson didn't divulge that information did he."

"You're right, I wonder now what Captain Lowe is going to say." Agent Haines stated.

"Me to." Jolene replied.

"So, I guess we're going there next?" Agent Blay asked.

CHAPTER 7

They loaded up in the car and were off to the forensic building. Jolene was ready for him. He couldn't deny what they had already learned. It was only five minutes away.

Pulling into the parking lot, Agent Haines turned to Jolene and spoke.

"Yes, I know. Keep my cool and don't hassle him or show anger." Jolene told him before he could start.

"Jolene, I know you and if you start, well, I'll tell you we have to leave." Agent Haines proclaimed.

They walked into the building and were confronted by one tech. "Can I help you?"

"Yes, we need to see Captain Lowe. Is he available?"

"I don't know. I'll call him. Who do I say is asking?"

"We're from the FBI." They all pulled out their badges to show him.

"Oh my, I'll call him right away."

"Please tell him it won't take long."

"I'll take you to his office. Boy, we've never had the FBI come here before. It must be pretty serious." He asked. He wanted to know more about their reason for seeing him, but they followed him silently.

Knocking on the Captain's door, he heard him say come in.

The captain stood up to greet them. "I'm Captain Lowe. What can I do for the FBI?"

"I'm Agent Johnson; this is Agent Haines and Agent Blay. We need to ask you about a case you were called in to investigate in Albany. There was also one in Malta."

"Alright, do you have a case number?" He asked.

"No, but I'm sure you will remember the case. It involved two women who were found in the local parks. They had been killed by their jugular on both sides had been cut, they were nude and bound with rope." Jolene was talking usually normally and not raising her voice.

"Oh yes, this was some time ago, like several years ago, right?"

"Sir, you are correct. It was sent to the FBI as a cold case, and that's why we're investigating it." Jolene stated.

"Let me look in my files. We keep everything on file we investigate." He replied.

Several minutes passed, and he returned with a folder in his hand.

"Okay, what can I tell you? Everything should have been in their file when it was sent over to the FBI."

"That's why we're here. There are several things that appear to be missing from the file we received." Agent Haines spoke up.

"I can make copies of our reports if that will help. It was a terrible thing to see. Their bodies were nude, and they were tied up with rope. They also had besides the incisions on their neck, there was damage to their breast."

"Did your team comb the surrounding area to see if anything was found, like blood or any other debris?" Jolene asked.

"Yes, we did. Nothing was found in the area or in the surrounding area. We wanted to go back the next day, but Detective Hudson told us it wasn't necessary."

"Did you take him at his word?" Agent Blay asked.

"Kind of. I told my team we were going back and check it out. There had to be something we were missing. I even had them check the local dumpsters in the area."

"Did they find anything of use?" Jolene asked.

"We did, but not sure if it belonged to the victims or not." Was his answer.

"What was it you found?" Jolene asked.

"We found burnt clothing and a couple of handbags. They hadn't completely burned. There were no contents in the bags. I told my team to comb through the bends carefully to see if there were any papers or pieces of paper which might have been part of the victims."

"Did they find anything?' Agent Blay spoke up.

"Here is a picture of what we found. Several pieces of clothing, several pieces of paper. The paper was burnt too bad to see what it contained."

"What about the clothing? Did it look like it might have been from someone in the neighborhood?" Jolene asked.

"Most of the people living in that area, well, they are all senior citizens. I don't believe they would have been wearing fancy clothes with sequins."

"So, you found parts of clothing which contained sequins?" Agent Haines was interested in knowing.

"Yes, because of the sequins, the clothing didn't burn completely. The sequins kept them from burning. They just melted together. Here is a picture of the clothing we found."

"Did you notify Detective Hudson about your findings?" Jolene was starting on a roll.

"Yes, we called him and gave him a copy of our report with the photographs."

"Did he comment about your findings?"

"The only thing I can remember was he told me to bury it. It wasn't important, and it was someone's belongings that were cleaning out their closet."

"Did your team go around and question some neighbors in the area? They must have seen the fire in the dumpster?" Jolene asked.

"We were going to, but didn't want to step on Detective Hudson's toes. We talked to a gentleman by the name of Joe. I can't remember his last name."

"He lived right across from the park, right?"

"Yes, he was the only one we talked to. He told us he saw the lady being dumped in the park. The dumpster was only a block away from the park."

"Did you take his statement?" Agent Haines asked.

"Yes, and I told him he should go to Detective Hudson with his statement. He became agitated and walked away. He had some type of run-in with Detective Hudson. Thats why he walked away."

"You would be correct. He is something like the neighborhood watch for the area. Detective Hudson has called him a meddling pest and didn't want to talk to him about anything anymore."

"You're kidding, right?" Captain Lowe stated.

"Yes, he was the one who called the police station disguising his voice when he saw the guy dumping the body. Joe said if he hadn't, they wouldn't have come."

"I thought something was wrong. Why would he give Joe a hard time?" He asked.

"From Joe, he had called the police several times about different things. They didn't want to know about it, like the punks who spray-painted the trees and buildings."

"I noticed the trees the following day. They have defaced almost all of them in the park. The building also had been sprayed with black and red paint. They had been tagged by some gang."

"See, that's what Joes up against. The police can't be bothered, according to Detective Hudson. His philosophy is this part of town was going to be replaced and these building will be removed."

"Oh, I see. You are right. The town is growing fast. They are tearing down these old places and building shopping malls. Which is a shame, for this was our heritage."

"Have you lived here for very long?" Jolene asked.

"I have, and Joe was always looking out for us kids. He never married. He would be out at the bus stop to make sure we got on and off. When there were bullies around, he would chase them off. Like I said, he was always looking out for us kids."

"So, you know him pretty well." Jolene stated.

"Yes, and the neighbors will miss him dearly when he's gone." Captain Lowe stated with his head nodding back and forth.

"Thank you for your honesty and the information. The copies will help with our investigation. I have one more question for you, the woman found in Malta. You did the investigation there also?" Jolene asked.

CHAPTER 8

"Yes, I've put our findings in the file I gave you. The only difference was there weren't any burnt articles in any dumpster there. Everything else was the same. The clothing items we found here were more than one person. I figure it was both of their clothing. There was a belt buckle also in the dumpster, but it was pretty charred along with some white material. It was pretty burnt as well."

The Agents stood up and extended their hands to shake his. They left with more information than they had, and now they had some of the missing pieces to the puzzle. Now, they had to put them together.

When they loaded up in the car and went back to the small cafe for coffee and discuss the findings. They had from Captain Lowe. Agent Haines had to compliment Jolene in keeping it cool.

"See Jolene, that's what makes you an outstanding agent!" Agent Haines stated.

Jolene was eager to get home. She wanted Agent Haines and Blay to return to his apartment, for she had to research Malta and what goes on there. It had to be something that caused the three ladies to go there. She was sure they were together at the time of their death. But she kept asking herself what was the answer. Did they travel there together? Did they meet after they had arrived? What about a vehicle? Did anyone report an abandoned car? These were unanswered questions.

"Jolene, what are you thinking? Do you want to run everything over with us?" Agent Haines asked.

"No, not right now. I need to do some research like I told you. Tomorrow, when I have some answers, we'll go over them then." Jolene answered.

Jolene knew she could run everything over her father, and he could tell her if she was on the right trail or if she should look at it differently.

"Boy Jolene, you ran them off rather early. Is everything alright?" Chief asked.

"Yes, Dad, I just wanted to be alone tonight. There are still a lot of unanswered questions."

"Oh, that's not like you to tell them to go away. Is there something I can help you with?" He asked.

"Yes, I was hoping I could run something by you. I don't know if I'm on the right track or not."

"Oh? You know you can use me for a sounding board. I've been following where you are on the board. It looks like you're doing a great job." Chief announced.

"I have a couple of things I want to research, and then if you can listen to me for a couple of minutes, you can give me your opinion."

"Okay, but I know your couple of minutes. I'm going to make some dinner and then we can talk."

"Great, what are we having?" Jolene asked.

"How about a TV dinner?"

"You're kidding, right?" Jolene said, laughing.

"No, I have beef or turkey. Which do you prefer?"

"I'll take the Turkey." Jolene replied.

While he put them in the oven, Jolene started her research. Jolene started with the impound yards. She was looking for any vehicles brought in five years ago with no owner claiming them. All she found was the cars brought in more that two years ago, had been junked and crushed. No owners' papers were removed from them.

"Jolene, dinner is ready."

"Coming dad. You know I believe in the police, but when they abuse their power and act like they don't care. I can't help it but get upset, dad. I know they all have a hard job to do, but I never heard you complain about our police persons or our two detectives. They all do their jobs and seem to be happy working for you."

"Yes, I know, honey. But you have to remember, not all the police departments are like ours. We're family and we treat each other like family. If one of them has a problem, well, we try to fix it."

"Thanks dad. I'm going to bed. The guys will be over early in the morning for us to go over everything."

"Okay, sleep tight." He gave her a kiss on the cheek.

The next morning, sharp at seven, they were at Jolene's door. This time, they brought coffee with the donuts. Both agents plainly saw that Jolene was pleased with what she had discovered. They were impressed with Jolene because she hadn't lost her temper. She had been very calm in her questions to Captain Lowe.

"Look, I don't care about that! You and Agent Blay give me the courage to do the things I do. Yes, I get upset when I don't get answers, and I know you guys do as well." Jolene replied.

"That's what makes us a great team together." Agent Blay put his two cents in.

"Sounds good to me. Do you think we need to go to Malta?" Agent Blay asked.

"Yes, I think we need to go there and check it out. We can leave now and be back by dinner. There has to be a reason all three women were killed, and I believe it is a night spot there. Although nobody has said anything about Malta."

"Do you suppose there was some type of concert there they all went to?" Agent Blay asked.

"Oh my, you're beginning to think like me!"

"Yeah, he is, and we better be careful or he'll be reading our minds all the time!" Agent Haines stated, and they all broke out and laughed.

"That's not fair, guys!" Agent Blay protested.

"Hey, that's a good thing. That way Jolene has a backup when she loses her temper." Agent Haines said.

"I don't lose my temper!" Jolene argued.

"Hey, we need to call your father and ask him if Jolene loses her temper." Agent Haines suggested to Jolene.

"Yes, we should. My cell phone has died. Agent Blay, give me your cell."

"Okay, how come your cell is dead?" He asked.

"I forgot to charge it last night. I was using it for research along with my computer."

"You know you can charge it while being on it, right?" Blay told her.

"Look, don't give me a hard time. Yes, I know, but I wasn't near an outlet, smarty." Jolene answered.

"Hi dad, just to let you know we may not be home tonight. But, let's go for spaghetti dinner when we get home?" Jolene suggested.

Agent Haines had to compliment Jolene in keeping it cool. They were on there was a home for the night. Jolene needed to call her dad and tell him they were on their way.

"See Jolene, that's what makes you an outstanding agent!" Agent Haines stated.

"Sounds good to me. Do you what me to pick it up on the way home?"

"No, we'll all go out to that Italian restaurant you know, Louie's. We'll meet you there. We're on the way home."

"Jolene, why are you calling me from Agent Blay's phone? Is something wrong with your phone?"

"Dad mine died, so I'm using his. He never uses it anyway." Jolene remarked.

"Hey that isn't true!" Blay said, loud enough for Chief Johnson to hear.

"I'm always telling her to plug it in." Chief said.

"Look, you guys quit picking on me!" Jolene said in retaliation. "I'll call you when we start headed home, or if we decide to stay the night in Malta, dad."

"Okay, I'll be waiting to hear from you."

When they were within five minutes of the restaurant, Jolene called her dad. To her surprise, he was there and had got a table.

They walked in and saw him right away. "Hi, Dad. How long have you been here?" Jolene asked.

"I just got here about five minutes ago. I know you were going to call me, but I figured when you arrive, I'd went ahead get a table."

"Thank you, Chief." Agent Haines stated.

"Well?" Chief said.

"Well, what, Dad?"

"How did it go?'

"Did you find any answers?" He asked.

Agent Blay jumped in with both feet. "You should have been there. Jolene raked a detective over the coals in fine style!"

"She didn't really!" Agent Haines commented.

"In my defense, I just told him the way I felt about his apathetic attitude toward the victims." Jolene raised her voice a little.

"Hey, okay, settle down!" Her father instructed.

"Sorry."

"See, just bringing it up and she shows you how it was." Agent Blay said.

"Look, I know how she is, and it must have been pretty bad for her to lose on the detective." Chief stated.

"It's like this, if she hadn't put him in his place. I would have." Agent Haines told him.

Jolene looked at him with a surprised look in her eyes. She hadn't realized he felt like her about the detective's attitude. It made her feel good about herself.

"We found out a lot. We met a man named Joe, and he was accommodating. Then we spoke to Captain Lowe with the forensic team. He was so helpful and gave us the missing parts of the case the detective didn't know about. Or he said nothing about."

"Now, what is the next step?" Chief asked.

"I'm going to do some more research tonight and see if there was any type of event in Malta these ladies could have gone to. It appears they were there for something. I just have to tie it together." Jolene stated.

"Tomorrow we'll be traveling to Malta and talk to the local bars in the area. Hopefully, they will add some missing items to this case." Agent Haines replied.

"You know there are several towns in the area up there which have events all the time. Special music events, and such." Chief told them.

"That's what I'm looking for. The bartenders could shed some light on these events and recognize these women." Jolene added. "Come on, guys let's eat." Their food just arrived at their table.

The aroma of the food made Agent Blay's mouth water. "Yes, let's eat. It smells so good." He announced.

Jolene was eager to get home. She wanted Agent Haines and Blay to return to his apartment, for she had to research Malta and what goes on there. It had to be something that caused the three ladies to go there. She was sure they were together at the time of their death. But she kept asking herself what was the answer. Did they travel there together? Did they meet after they had arrived? These were unanswered questions.

"Jolene, what are you thinking? Do you want to run everything over with us?" Agent Haines asked.

"No, not right now. I need to do some research like I told you. Tomorrow when I have some of the answer's we'll go over them then." Jolene answered.

She had put Malta on the board with a question mark and also Bolton Springs with a question mark. This was puzzling to her father.

"Okay, dinner is served." He announced.

Meanwhile, her computer was working over-time while they ate.

The research showed that Malta had a big music festival in the second week of March and a gigantic flea market. It offered music bands from many types of music. The flea market was on the main street and lasted for several blocks. People from all over came to it.

Bolton Springs was only forty-five minutes away on Highway Nine. It was also a tourist attraction with hiking and a memorial park on the lake. It also housed a large convention center hosting greetings for several corporations.

They were one of the most sought-after music festivals for convenience. Five to six years ago, there was a convention for news reporters for approximately one hundred and fifty attendees.

"Okay. Dad, I might be on the right track. These women were in Bolton Springs at the convention. Even though nobody recognized the photographs of the women, Captain Lowe said there were burnt items in a dumpster."

"Okay, Jolene, why would the killer bring the bodies back to Malta, Albany, and Troy?" He asked.

"I haven't figured that out yet. I ordered some instruments online. And they will be here tomorrow." Jolene announced.

"What instruments?"

"Just a couple of things, a couple of scalpels and aplastic surgeon's laser instrument."

"Jolene, have a medical license to buy that kind of stuff!"

"Dad, believe it or not, there was no identification required. I could buy as much as I wanted."

"But how did you come up with these being the murder weapons?"

"The medical examiner said the incisions on both sides of their necks were approximately the same length on each body, and the instrument used couldn't have been a knife. The breast tissue removal was cauterized as the incision was made in perfect circumference. There was no bleeding from the breast on any of the women. Only the incisions on the neck."

"Was there any blood found at the scene?"

"No, it appeared the bodies had been dumped in the parks independently. Joe saw the one being dumped in Albany, but couldn't tell if there was another body in the trunk of his car."

"So, why do you think these women went to the music festival or Bolton Springs?"

"It kind of makes sense because if they were news casters, they may have been covering the festival and then went on to the news conference in Bolton Springs, doesn't it?"

"Jolene, trust your gut. It appears you have drawn your conclusions from what you have learnt so far." Dad was being supportive.

"But Dad, you don't think I'm being a little presumption, do you?"

"No, but I believe you are still aways from deciding on who the killer is."

"Yes, like I want to question the medical doctor in Malta. He is supposed to be an eminent physician and knows everything. This includes surgery. I did a background on him."

"Who is this doctor?"

Having earned his medical degree in China, he hails from there. Following that, he moved to New York and pursued his surgical residency at the University. He's been in the States for twenty years. He settled in Malta about fifteen years ago. There is an enormous gap in his practice for about two years. No other information was available."

"Then you are going to Malta to question him?"

"Yes, that's our next move and then on to Bolton Springs. They should have a list of attendees for the conferences, and I'm hoping we will find some more information there." Jolene said with a sigh.

"Before you leave, run all of this by Agent Haines and see what he thinks. I know he backs you up with whatever you want to do. You're on the right track. I just want him to be with you."

"Thanks, Dad."

"Jolene, just be careful. Don't put yourself in harm's way. If this doctor is the killer, I'm not saying he is, but if he is, he could make you his next target."

"Yes, Dad. There have been no other killings with the same MO that we know of. The problem is if he's still out there killing, we won't know it until it becomes a cold case. Then it's too late!"

"Jolene you can't think like that." Chief scolded her.

"Good night, Dad. I'm tired and going to bed."

"Get some rest, and tomorrow will look clearer."

The following day, Jolene was up at four AM. She stared at the blackboard and wondered if she needed to remember something. Jolene looked over at the clock on the wall and saw it was going on six. She couldn't wait any longer, so she picked up the phone and called Agent Haines.

"Agent Haines, sorry to call you so early, but we need to go over everything this morning before we leave for Malta."

"Okay, but the sun isn't up yet! Can you wait for a couple more hours?"

"I guess, but really, a couple of hours? Let's say in an hour? Agree? Jolene begged.

"Alright, Jolene. Something must have you wound up." He knew he couldn't win by arguing.

Agent Haines woke up Agent Blay, who started grumbling about the hour. Once he told him Jolene needed them immediately, he jumped up and was in the shower.

They drove over to Jolene's and jumped out of the car. Chief looked out the window and announced, "the boys are here. Did you call them this morning?"

"Sorry, Dad, I called them to come over. We have a lot of information to review. Plus, the theory I gave you last night."

"Come in, boys! My crazy daughter is inside!"

"Chief, have the coffee on?"

"Coming right up. I just got up myself. She's so quiet until she wants something, then you can't get her to be quiet."

"Come on, Dad!"

They sat around the table and listened carefully to what Jolene had to say. She pointed out everything on the board. She even told them her theory.

Agent Haines agreed with Jolene. He had nothing to say. After they drank their coffee. Jolene looked over at Agent Blay.

"Why are you so quiet?" She asked.

"Well, it's time for breakfast, isn't it?"

All of them began laughing. Blay was always hungry!

There was a knock on the door. It was eight o'clock.

"I'll get it, dad."

The delivery was for Jolene. It was the medical instruments she had ordered. She hadn't told Agent Haines of Blay about those yet."

"So, let's see what's in the box Jolene?" Chief said.

Jolene opened the box carefully. Inside was exactly what she had ordered. A forty- piece surgical scalpel set and one electric cauterizing scalpel. They watched her lay all of them out on the table.

"What in the world? What is all of this?" Agent Haines asked.

"Believe it or not. I ordered these when I got home to be delivered this morning before nine. It was delivered on time and I didn't have to prove I was a physician or surgeon to order them." Jolene said, boosting.

"Come on, you would have had to give them some type of license?"

"Nope, I just picked up the phone, gave them the order number and the address where to deliver them. They told me how much I paid with a credit card and my order was processed."

"So now what, we're going to try them out?" Agent Blay asked.

"Well, I thought about that. There has to be something we can try them out on. Some type of fruit, maybe? What do you think, Dad?"

"You should talk to our medical examiner. She would know what to use them on and not a body, I pray."

"Good idea, Dad. Do you think she's in her office this morning?"

"She should be in. Let me call her first and tell her you're coming. If I don't, she might think you're a nut!"

Chief picked up his cell phone and dialed her number. On the second ring, she answered.

"Hello, Mavis, this is Chief Johnson. I have a favor to ask you."

"Yes, Chief Johnson, what can I do for you?'

"My daughter wants to come by and talk with you. Her two FBI agents will be with her. I appreciated all the help you can give her."

"Not a problem, Chief Johnson. I'm going to be tied up for about an hour, but after that, I'll be available." Dr. Mavis Henderson stated.

"Thank you." They both hung up.

"Okay Jolene, Dr. Henderson said she could see you in an hour. Be gentle with her. She is an expert. Be sure to take your new toys with you."

"Maybe we can donate them to her after you finish with your experiment." Agent Haines told her.

It was only fifteen minutes away, but she wouldn't be available for an hour. Now, they had to kill time before they could see her. Since they hadn't had breakfast, they went to the local café in town. This would appease Agent Blay, for he had already mentioned he was hungry.

"Now that we have fed you, are you ready to go to the morgue?" Jolene looked at Blay.

"Go to the morgue? You mean where all those bodies are kept?"

Agent Haines couldn't help but laugh at him. It wasn't like he hadn't seen a dead body before. This would be the first time they did autopsies, and that was something he hadn't experienced yet.

"Hello, we're here?"

"Hello, you must be Jolene."

"Yes, the chief called you this morning."

"Yes, I just love that man. What can I do for you, Jolene?"

"First, this is Agent Haines and Agent Blay. I've brought some toys to play with and I need your expertise in determining which one is better for the job."

"Oh, I see. Let me see what you have?"

Jolene spread them out on the table for her to see. She was very impressed with her selection.

"Jolene, may I ask you what you are trying to do with these?"

"We're working on a murder case. The carotid arteries were cut precisely one and one-half inches, and both were exact. Both measured the same. The wounds were not jagged, so we know it couldn't have been made with a knife."

"Well, then I would have used this handle with this blade. It's thin and exact to the point. The dimensions of the width of the blade would make it look like a paper cut."

"Great! That's what I needed. We now have the instrument we're looking for. What about this one?" Jolene pulled out the other one.

"Boy, you came well equipped!"

"What about it? Could it be used to cut of the breast of the breast and keep them from bleeding?"

"You got it. It's used to cauterize the tissue to keep it from bleeding. It's used under anesthesia by surgeons to keep the wound clean. Were there sutures where they removed the breast?"

"Yes, it was a fine gut suture material, very precise in the stitching."

"Thank you, Doctor. You have been a big help." Jolene raised her hand to shake hers.

"May I ask you where you received these from?"

"I ordered them on line. Dad said I could donate them to you. I don't think I'll need them again, but if I do, I know where to come to and borrow them back." Jolene said.

"You are kidding me, right?"

"No, ma'am."

Agent Haines shook her hand and smiled.

They walked out, and Jolene was smiling ear to ear. She now knew what was used in the murders. Agent Blay looked at Jolene with wonder in his eyes.

"Jolene, I have to ask you a question."

"Okay, shoot."

"How do you know so much, or how did you know you could order these things without a license?"

"It's like this. The medical examiner said he couldn't determine what instrument was used. He said it wasn't any type of knife he knew of. The blade would have made a wider incision and been jagged."

"The incision to remove the breast on the breast was clean, with no bleeding from them. That meant it had to be something that could cut and cauterizing the incision."

"Yes, I understand that, but how did you know to look for surgical instruments?"

"I thought about what a surgeon would use, maybe a plastic surgeon. So, I began looking up special instruments they would use."

"The rest is history." Jolene said with a smile on her face.

"Okay, I guess we're off to Malta?" Agent Haines asked.

"On Silver, on dancer and on Pancer!"

They loaded up, and we're off. Agent Haines was very impressed with all the information Jolene had put on the board. He also knew she had become up with the type of weapon used. Now they had to find who the plastic surgeon used for them.

"Jolene, where are we going first in Malta?"

"They have two bars, one named 'Beer R Us' and the other one 'Drink A Lot'. We can start there first. Then I thought we could talk to the mayor."

"Are you sure you don't want to talk to the mayor first?" Agent Blay asked.

"I think we'll probably get more information from the bartenders than the major. He's going to just tell us what a fine town he has and how much the festival does for his town. Bla, bla, bla, wait and see."

"I know the festival is good for the town and its people. Many small towns hold things like this once a year and profit big from the tourists that attend."

"We need to talk to their doctor after the mayor. I'll be interested in seeing where he was during this festival and what he did during that two-year missing time."

"Missing time?" Agent Haines asked.

"Yes, when I was checking him out, well, he disappeared for about twenty-four months prior to taking the job at Malta. There wasn't any trace for that time." Jolene stated.

"Was he already hired to come to Malta as their primary physician?" Agent Haines asked.

"Yes, he took the job, and told them he won't be able to come to their town for two years." Jolene stated.

"Oh, so he left to go somewhere, but there is no record where he went." Agent Blay asked.

"Yes."

"It'll be interesting to find out." Agent Haines Stated.

"Let's have some lunch before we dig in to the bars." Agent Blay asked.

"Sounds good to me. There is supposed to be a small Café just at the edge of town. We could try it." Agent Haines stated.

"Oh my, you know we're to eat for a change?" Blay asked.

"Hey, I do research too, you know."

"Yeah, it's going on eleven, so lunch is a good idea."

They pulled into the parking lot and saw several cars already there. They wondered why so many people would be there that early?

Jolene was very impressed. It was spotless, and the tables were setup with everything they would need. The tables even had place mats. They were made of paper towels. This was unusual, but it worked.

"Just have a seat anywhere." The waitress told them. It only took her a minute before she was standing there at their table. We'll have three cups of coffee." Jolene started. "Do you have menus?" She asked.

"It's on the blackboard."

They looked at the board. Bowl Chili, Hamburger with fries. Both were one dollar and twenty-five cents. Agent Blay started first. "I'll have the chili."

Jolene ordered the hamburger and fries. Agent Haines told her he'd have the same as Jolene. She told them thank you and removed the extra place mat.

It only took a few minutes for their food to arrive. It was served on thick paper plates and the chili in a paper bowl. Agent Blay was sure it would go through the paper, but he didn't realize the bowl was plastic lined so it couldn't leak through.

They took their time eating. The only complaint they heard was from Agent Blay. The chili was so hot it burnt his mouth. Not only was it hot, but the spices were scorching.

They asked for another cup of coffee and Agent Blay asked for two glasses of water! Jolene and Agent Haines couldn't help but laugh at him.

Jolene asked her a couple of questions while Agent Blay cooled his mouth down.

When she brought back the coffee and the water, Jolene thought that would be the perfect time.

Her name tag stated her name was Eva. "Hello Eva, can I ask you a couple of questions?"

"Sure. What would you like to know?"

"Eva, have you lived in Malta for very long?"

"Yeah, most of my life. My husband and I moved to her when we got married, about fifteen years ago. We lived in Albany before moving here. It was just to crowed and busy for us. Here in Malta is just right."

"So, you know most people here?"

Yes, I guess so. Everyone is so nice here and friendly. We have our own doctor and all, so we don't have to go anywhere when we get sick or need medical attention."

"What do most of the people do around here for jobs?" Agent Haines asked.

"We have a couple of mills, and there were plenty of farms, dairy and chicken. Are you folks looking to move here?" She asked.

"We're just looking around." Agent Blay quickly added.

"Oh, I'm sure you and your wife and your father would absolutely love it here." Eva announced.

Jolene started blushing. If she only knew who we really were! She thought.

Agent Haines asked her for the bill. Which Eva gave to him. It came to five dollars and twenty-five cents. He couldn't believe the check. He gave her the exact amount for the bill and left her a tip of five dollars.

"Oh my, thank you, sir. I hope you folks move here. It's nice people like you that are appreciated here." Eva stated.

Agent Haines raised his hand and politely waved.

When they were in the car, Agent Haines looked at Blay and said, "They also serve breakfast."

"Oh yeah"

"Two eggs, bacon or pork sausage, and hash browns, with toast or biscuit for a dollar and fifty cents." Agent Haines announced.

"Hey, that will give you incentive to move here, now doesn't it, Pop?"

"Just for your information, I wouldn't be your pop if you paid me to be!" Agent Haines stated, then he laughed.

Jolene was laughing so hard she had tears running down her face. "But you would be my pop, wouldn't you?" She asked.

"Why sure, it wouldn't cost an arm and a leg to feed you!" He stated.

CHAPTER 9

"Okay, let's head over to the Doctor Woneg office. He's probably seeing patients, so we'll have to be patient." Jolene announced.

"Yes, and he may put us off. We'll have to let him know we're not leaving until he speaks to us." Agent Haines announced.

"We can use the excuse I'm not feeling too well. I think that chili is fighting with my guts!" Agent Blay stated.

"Hey, that's a great in! You're not feeling well, really?" Jolene asked.

"I've eaten chili before, but I tell you, this is not agreeing with me." Blay had a look on his face that told the entire story.

"We'll be at his office in a couple of minutes, so try to hang in there." Agent Haines told him.

They parked the car and helped Agent Blay inside Doctor Woneg's office. The receptionist looked at Agent Blay and said, "this way."

Jolene and Agent Haines followed her as she helped Agent Blay to an exam room. "I'll tell the Doctor you're here. He'll be in just a couple of minutes."

Jolene was impressed at how clean the office was and how it appeared to be running efficiently. They heard the doctor coming.

"Hello, I understand you have a tummy ache?" He asked.

Agent Blay just nodded his yes.

"I bet you ate the chili over at the café, right?"

"How did you know?" Agent Haines asked.

"The first timers always end up here. Don't get me wrong, it's good chili, but you have to grow accustom to it slowly."

"Isn't there something you can give him to help?" Jolene broke into the conversation.

"Oh yes, we'll have him back to his old self in no time."

They started I.V.'s and gave him some medicine for them. He was feeling better in a few minutes. The Doctors advise was for him to stay away from the chili at the café.

"Doctor Woneg, we would like to ask you a few questions if you could give us a few minutes." Jolen asked.

"Sure, but like I said, you husband will be fine."

Let me clarify, he is not my husband. I'm Agent Johnson. This is Agent Haines, and the patient is Agent Blay. We are with the FBI."

"Oh, I see. What can I do for you?"

"Several years ago, there was a young woman found in your park. Do you remember this?"

"Yes, I think so. She was murdered, if I remember correctly. That's what the police said."

"We're trying to find out as much as we can about her murder. We believe she was here for the big festival you have in town." Jolene said.

"I don't remember the details, but I was called to the scene when they found her. There wasn't anything I could do, for she was deceased." Doctor Woneg answered.

"During the festival, do you walk around and see the crowds of people?" Agent Haines asked.

"Yes, the festival is quite something, with all the music and the vendors with their booths of merchandise for sale. The town people come out in all their glory."

"Do you remember seeing this woman in the crowds of people, anything that might have to stand out about her?"

"No, I don't recall. It's been several years and there have been several festivals since then."

"Okay, I noticed you went to China for your medical degree. Then you came to the United States to finish your internship and residency. Is that correct?" Jolene asked.

"Yes, that's the truth."

"Before you took this job as their medical doctor, you disappear for a couple of years. Do you mind if I ask you where you were?"

"I went back to my homeland to study." Doctor Woneg answered.

"What did you study?"

"I studied plastic surgery. I wanted to repair any lacerations or repair anybody that might want the removal of any moles or small tumors they might have. Many of these people don't want to travel to Albany to the hospital if it's something I can do here in the office."

"So, you have the room that is surgically sterile to complete this type of surgery?" Jolene asked.

"Yes, I could show it to you. But you can't go in the room itself."

"I would like to see what type of setup you have, if you don't mind." Jolene was pushing.

"Come this way." He showed them the way.

Agent Haines and Jolene looked. It looked very impressive.

"What do you do if you have to sedate someone?" Jolene asked.

"I have a person who helps me. She is trained in anesthesia and is board certified. She has worked for me for the past three years."

"Does she do anything else for you here in the office?" Agent Haines asked.

"She also draws blood and does my lab test here. Instead of sending it to the lab in Albany, it's more cost effective."

"Thank you for your time." Agent Haines shook his hand, and Jolene extended her hand as well.

"I believe your agent should be ready to leave now. I'll check on him."

"Great!" Jolene said.

He called his nurse to remove his IV and give him some medicine to take with him.

"Remember, no chili from the cafe!"

"We'll make sure of that! What is the bill for your services today?" Agent Haines asked.

"Oh, there's no charge. We get these in here all the time. You can contribute."

"Sure, we will. We appreciate your help."

"Jolene, let's collect Agent Blay and move on."

"That's fine with me."

It was two o'clock, and Jolene wanted to hit the bars. She knew it was probably hopeless, but maybe someone would remember something.

The first one was called Beer R Us. The place already looked like it might be packed. It was too early for the workers to be out of work this early,

The three of them walked in and up to the bar. It wasn't crowded at all. The bartender came over to take their order.

"Give us three beers." Agent Haines ordered.

"Can we ask you a few questions?" Jolene was already starting.

"Sure, what do you want to know, pretty lady."

"How long have you lived here in Malta?"

"I've been here all my life. This is my bar. I started it when I was twenty-five years old and I've made it what it is today."

"Great, but what I want to know, have you seen this woman? It would have been about five years ago." Jolene put a picture of her on the bar.

"No, I can't say I do. Now, if she came in like you, I would have remembered."

"It might have been during one festival you have in town." Agent Haines asked.

"Honey, there are so many people during our shin-dig I wouldn't recognize my mother!"

"Thank you." Agent Haines threw a ten-dollar bill on the bar, and they walked out.

"Well, that was useless! We'll probably get the same story at the next bar," Jolene announced.

"I hope he doesn't flirt with you like this guy!" Agent Blay stated.

"Oh, come on, don't tell me you were jealous!"

Agent Haines looked at Jolene and snickered.

"Okay, let's get serious. The bar is supposed to be just up the road. Drinks a lot! What a name!"

They walked in and immediately were addressed.

"Welcome, FBI agents! What can I get yeah?"

"Nothing right now. We would like to ask you a few questions."

"Sure, let's go to my office."

"How did you know we're FBI agents?" Agent Blay asked.

"The owner of Beer R Us called me and told me you were probably on your way over here. He said to look for the cute chick, that would be the FBI."

"Everybody here knows everyone's business. So, what did you want to ask me?"

Jolene laid out the pictures of all three women. She could tell he knew something.

"Did you know these women?"

"They were here for the big music festival. They spent most of the night here, for they said they liked the music. We had better."

"Did you get their name?" Jolene asked.

"No, it was so crowded here I couldn't keep up with myself. The only reason I remember the women is they were together, and they were asking questions about Bolton Springs."

"What questions?" Agent Haines asked.

"One of them said they had a conference to attend there. They wanted to know how far it was to get there and was there a motel close they could stay at for the night. All our motels and hotels were full. They had booked nothing in advance."

"Did you give them some details as to where they could stay?" Jolene asked.

"I told them Saratoga Springs was only a few minutes away. They might have some rooms still available."

"It's simple amazing you remember so much about them!" Jolene stated.

"I have a glorious memory. I'm also in the fire rescue department. Once the one lady was found we were called to the scene, then the Doctor."

"Thanks." Jolene said.

CHAPTER 10

We won't have any luck going to Saratoga Springs. They have guests all year round and would need to remember three women traveling alone. They are a stopping-off place for people traveling on vacation.

Our best chances are to travel to Bolton Springs and see what we can find. They would have records of seminars they have had in the past. We might find out who was in charge of the seminar five years ago and who attended.

"But Jolene, you are looking at over a hundred people that attended the seminar. We can't interview all of them?"

"No, just ninety-seven of them!" Jolene replied.

"You have to be kidding!" Agent Blay answered.

"Look, our best chances are to see who attended and if they actually got to the seminar or not." Jolene stated.

"She's right. If they didn't make it to the seminar, then we know who we're looking for." Agent Haines replied.

"That will give us the names of the women. Then we can find out where they came from and if they have any family there." Jolene was right on the money.

"We know the seminar was for real estate brokers. So, whoever put the seminar on has a list of all the attendees. Hopefully, we can get a list of those who attended. If the women attended the seminar, then we know they were still alive."

"But if they attended, how is that going to help us?" Agent Blay asked.

"They would have had a room there, so if everyone checked out, and if they stayed on because of the attractions there, they would have left their luggage. The manager of the motel would have kept it just in case they returned for it." Jolene said.

"How do you know they would have kept it?" Agent Blay asked.

"They wouldn't want to throw away a person's luggage and having to pay for the contents." Jolene answered.

"But how long would they keep it for?" He asked.

"Well, if they put it in the basement, it could be there for a long time. They would forget about it even being there." Agent Haines replied.

"Yes, that's what we're hoping for. It would give us the clue we're looking for." Jolene said.

They pulled into Bolton Springs around dark. It was a busy place. People were milling around the grounds. According to the visitors' information about the place, there was much to see and do.

"Jolene, where do you want to start?" Agent Haines asked.

"We need to check in and look around. We can find out who the manager is." Jolene said.

"Okay, and then can we find a place to eat?" Agent Blay was always looking for food.

"I thought after that episode with the chili you wouldn't want to see food any longer!" Jolene remarked.

"Hey, that was six hours ago!" His reply.

Agent Haines just laughed.

"Look, they probably have a dining room in the hotel. We'll check in and then feed you!"

"Great, I'm starved!"

"Hello, we'd like to check in." Agent Haines said.

"How many rooms would you like?" The desk clerk asked.

"That would be two rooms, please." Agent Haines requested.

"Please sign in on the register."

"Is there a lot to do around here?" Jolene asked.

"Oh yes, we have the Veterans Memorial Park, and there is mountain climbing if you're into that. We have a lovely park with picnic tables. But if you're considering getting one, you must claim it early, for they go fast!"

"Is the picnic area close to the park?" Agent Haines asked.

"The kitchen will pack you a lunch if you request. We also have a lake; you can rent a boat and do some fishing. If you want to just relax, you can sit by the pool."

"Gee, there is a lot to do!" Jolene remarked.

"I understand you also have seminars here?" Agent Haines threw in.

"Oh yes. We have seminars all year round. People come from all over to attend our seminars."

"Really, what type of seminars do you host here?" Jolene asked.

"All types like real estate, mortgage brokers, law enforcement, and many others."

"Is there a seminar going on now?"

"Not this week. You are very lucky, otherwise you wouldn't get a room. We are booked up when we're hosting a seminar."

"I guess we are lucky then." Agent Blay replied.

They took their luggage and went to their rooms. Jolene wanted to meet up and talk about what their next move would be.

"First, we need to check out the memorial. There would be a register log; we might see who came there. It was a long shot, but the registry would have gone back five years." Jolene said.

"Jolene, how are we going to compare the names to the attendees of the seminar?" Agent Haines asked.

"I'll photograph the names of the attendees and compare them to the attendees of the seminar. Which will give us a list of names we need to check out if any of them left their luggage."

"We'll talk to the manager of the hotel after we do that." Agent Haines replied.

"Why am I always left in the dark? You and Jolene have all the answers, and I feel like I'm always trying to catch up!" Agent Blay stated.

Jolene put her arms around him and looked him in the eyes. "Look, Agent Haines has been at this a long time and so have I. We're sorry you're always trying to catch up. but this is the way you learn the trade."

"Yes, and Jolene has been at this since she was a teenager. You were just introduced to us a year or two ago. There is nothing to feel you are behind in anything." Agent Haines explained.

"In a couple of years, you'll be giving us suggestions." Jolene tried to comfort him.

"Agent Haines, did you notice we were being tailed on the way up here?"

"Yes, that blue sedan?"

"Yes, I noticed when we stopped for gas. He was parked on the side of the road. As soon as we pulled out, he pulled out and began following us. I don't see his car anywhere here, did you?"

"What car? Following us? Who, when?" Agent Blay asked.

"You were in the back seat, so you wouldn't have seen him." Jolene stated.

"What type of car was it?" Agent Blay asked. He turned in the seat to see.

"Don't turn around Blay! We don't want him to know we know he's back there!" Jolene scolded him.

"It was a blue sedan, probably a late model two thousand and thirteen chevy." Agent Haines replied.

"Why would he be following us?" Agent Blay asked.

"That's a good question. We'll have to keep our eyes open to see if we can identify him." Jolene stated.

"What do we do if we identify the person?" Agent Blay asked.

"We will see why he's so interest in what our business is!" Agent Haines stated.

The following day, they headed for the Memorial. There was a curator. A keeper of the records for the Museum. He would keep the records of guests who attended the seminars, and the hotel would keep the records of guests who registered there.

"Let's walk around the Museum and see if we pick up a tail." Jolene stated.

They walked around slowly to see what popped out. It was fascinating to see all the memorabilia there. It was all dedicated to veterans from World War II to the present.

"If anyone wanted to learn anything about the war's this would be the place to go." Jolene stated.

"You're right. They have everything here and there doesn't seem to be anything missing." Agent Haines replied.

"You should know. Wasn't the second world war during your time?" Agent Blay was trying to be funny.

"Yeah!" Agent Haines replied.

"Agent Haines, do you see that guy in the blue jean jacket?" Jolene asked.

"Yes, he came in right after us. Let's jump over to the Veit Nam War. We'll see if he follows or turns the other way."

The person started looking down like he was reading something. Then he looked up to see if he was still caught up to them.

"Agent Blay, go back to exhibits and we'll go ahead."

"What do you want me to do?" Agent Blay asked.

"Take a couple of photographs of the exhibit and make sure you get a shot or two of our trackers." Jolene instructed.

"Then what?" He asked.

"Then meet up with us," Agent Haines told him.

Jolene noticed he didn't have a camera around his neck, and she didn't see a cell phone. This had to be the one following them. Now they had to wait for Agent Blay to catch up. They were going to go over to the park. They had ordered a packed lunch from the kitchen. So now they would pick out a table and have lunch.

"Did you get the picture?" Jolene asked.

"Send it to the home office and ask them to run it. I want to see if he has a criminal history to see what he's up to."

"Yes, it appears we've seen this person before. If I'm correct. We've seen him at the bar. Drink-A-Lot. Remember, he was sitting at the end of the bar."

"Sit over here next to me," Jolene requested.

"Yea, make it look like you two are a couple. I'm just grandfather tagging along for the ride." Agent Haines said.

"Okay, can we eat now?" Agent Blay requested.

"Oh my, always thinking of food!" Jolene stated loudly.

"I'll unpack the basket." Jolene told him.

"Hey pop, what do you want to do next?" Agent Blay asked.

They looked around and saw the man sitting two tables from where they were. Now was the perfect time to see who this was. If he was at the bar, he knew they were FBI agents.

"I need to use the restrooms. I'll be right back," Agent Haines announced.

He got up and moved toward the restrooms. Then he circled around behind the man. He placed his hand on his shoulder and which startled him. Jolene and Agent Blay hurried over to the table.

"Okay, what's your name?" Jolene jumped in with both feet.

"I'm a tourist, just like you," was his answer.

"I asked you what your name was?" Jolene said again.

"I'm Joe Brown." was his answer.

"Mr. Brown, why are you following us?" Agent Haines asked.

"I'm not following you. What do you mean?"

"Look, we saw you at the bar and you were following us all the way here. Everywhere we've gone, you are turning up." Agent Blay stated.

"I think we should call the police to hold him for twenty-four hours. What do you think, Jolene?"

"I believe that would be a great idea!"

"No, no, please don't. I'll tell you what I'm doing!"

"So, spit it out Mr. Brown." Agent Blay told him.

"I'm a reporter, and I heard you were looking for the killer of three women. It's a story I covered five years ago, and nobody would listen to me back then. I heard the FBI was looking into it. I thought maybe I'd tag along. I know it's an impossible case, but I know they were killed by a local!" He announced.

"I'm afraid I would like to see some credentials, so we can verify your story." Jolene requested.

"Sure, here is my press pass. I have done nothing wrong." He was pleading.

The cell phone started ringing, so Agent Haines answered it. "Hello, Agent Haines."

"Agent Haines, this is the agency. We've run the photograph you sent to us. We ran the photo, and it appears he is a news report. He usually works alone, and he becomes a nuisance to everyone, including the police!"

"Has he ever been arrested for anything else?" Agent Haines asked.

"Nothing on record. There was a report he was engaged about five years ago and appeared he was going to work for the New York times. The woman he was engaged to, apparently his bride to be, disappeared. It was rumored she pulled a Hank Snow."

"Thanks, Mickey. Like always, you come through for me." Agent Haines said and hung up.

"Alright, say we believe you. What is the real reason you are following us? Don't tell me it's for a story! One woman was your fiancé?" Agent Haines asked.

"Yes, I can't proof it was her." Mr. Brown stated.

"If I show you some photographs, you can tell if one of them was her."

"You have pictures?"

"Here, look at these and see if you recognize them?" Jolene stated as she pulled the photographs from her bag.

"Yes, this is Sharon!" He yelled out. "I knew something happened to her. These are her best friends, Judy and Ann." He became really excited.

"Do you have her best friend's last names?" Jolene asked.

"Judy Mida, Ann Fletcher, and Sharon Combs, we were to be married in the spring."

"The police won't let me see their bodies after they were found. I told them to identify themselves and they sent me away. They said there was no reason for me to see the bodies. I wasn't family and they wouldn't even take down their names just encase I was right!"

"So why didn't you get a hold of us?" Agent Blay asked.

"It didn't occur to me to reach out to the FBI. The police were handling the investigation." He stated. "I've waited five years now I have. I can get on with my life after I write this story."

"You said you were to marry in the spring?" Jolene asked.

"Yes, this trip was for Sharon. It was like a bridal shower for her. Like this was going to be her last hora before getting married. Mr. Brown added.

"This will give us something to go on. Can you give us the addresses of all them?" Jolene asked.

"Yes, they all lived in the same building. Their parents lived in the same town. They worked for the same real estate agency. They were going to start their own company after we were married. There was a building all ready for them to move in. They even had business cards printed. Here is one of them." He handed Jolene the business card.

"I went there twice, and then they told me not to come back the second time I went there! Scarlette, a friend of hers, told me she knew about them wanting to start their own business and the boss wasn't happy for she had heard about it. That's why she told me not to come back."

"So, her boss thought she had started her own agency. She probably thought you were there to steal clients for her." Jolene said.

"Maybe, but I would have never done that. But being a reported, who knows what she thought." Mr. Brown Stated.

"I knew she wouldn't have just left me. We were to be married the second week in April. Her best friends were her bride's maid. They were always getting together to talk about our wedding plans. If she was going to leave me, why would they get together and talk about our wedding plans? That just didn't make scents to me." Mr. Brown had tears running down his face.

"Look, we want you to go home. We'll keep you updated when we know more, and I promise you, when we make an arrest, you'll know." Agent Haines told him.

"We can't have you tailing us around. It could be dangerous. Promise us you will go home and wait for us to call you." Jolene was being very stern with him.

"Okay, but you promise you will let me know everything you do, and when you make an arrest, you will let me know?" Mr. Brown stressed.

"Yes, I promise," Agent Haines confirmed.

"We have to ask you not to tell the parents of the women. We'll do that. It wouldn't be good if you told them just yet. We will handle it in due time," Agent Blay added.

"Alright, I won't say anything. They have been worried to death about their daughters. They keep hoping they would call or come home." Mr. Brown stated.

"I know it has been hard for them as well. We're trying to do everything possible to track down their movements, and you have been a big help."

"We now have their names, which will help a great deal in what we're doing." Agent Haines concurred.

Mr. Brown stood up and hugged Jolene, Agent Haines, and Agent Blay. He appreciated them talking with him.

"Thank you for talking with me."

He left the park, and Agent Blay walked with him. He got in his car. It was a light blue Chevy. Agent Blay was excited to go back and tell Jolene and Haines about what car he was driving.

Agent Haines and Jolene had already figured that out but didn't want to hurt Agent Blay's feelings, so they said great. Now we know who was following us for sure.

The information they received from Mr. Brown was great. Now, they could check for their names to show up on the registries.

"We now know there was a breakaway from their current real estate company. They were supposed to attend the seminar for realtors. We'll see if they show up."

"I have the name of the company which puts on the seminar once a year. Lucky for us, it's always the same company that entertains these seminars. His name is Jack Harvey." Jolene stated.

"How do we find this, Mr. Harvey?" Blay asked.

"He's local here in town. He puts on several seminars here every year. I located his address. We'll go there next." Agent Haines stated.

As they loaded up in the car, Jolene suddenly remembered something.

"Hey fellows, we can check out the Memorial. They had to have signed in there before they could get in."

"You're right. We had to sign in before he would let us in. Let's walk over and see if we can get the records from five years ago around the time of the seminar."

They walked over to the Memorial, and the guard at the door looked at them like they were intruders.

"Hello, Mr. Wilson, we were here earlier, remember us?" Jolene asked.

"Yes, I remember you three. Why are you back again?" He asked.

"We, it's like this. We need to speak to the man in charge of this memorial." Jolene stated.

"That would be General Harvey. Do you know him?" The guard asked.

"No, we don't. But it's imperative we speak to him." Jolene whined a little so he would take them seriously.

"I'll call his office and see if he can speak to you. Just a minute. Don't move." He warned.

Jolene wondered why he was being so strict with them. They weren't there to steal anything. He walked back to where they were standing.

"General Harvey said he'd see you. Go to the yellow door. That is his office."

They followed his instructions and walked over to the yellow door, and Agent Haines knocked. They waited until they heard him say come in.

"Come in." as they walked in, he stood up. Mr. Harvey was dressed in a full army uniform with his medals pinned to his chest.

"Hello, General Harvey. I'm Agent Johnson, and this is Agent Haines, Agent Blay. We're from the FBI." They pulled out their badges to show him.

"What do I owe the honor of the FBI to see me?"

"We need to see your records from five years ago. There was a real estate seminar in the hall." Jolene replied.

"Sir, what branch of the military did you serve in?" Agent Blay asked.

"I was in the army for over thirty years." Was his reply.

"What was your position with the army?" Jolene asked.

"I was with the medical corp and a surgeon." General Harvey replied.

"I see you retired as a five-star general." Agent Haines stated.

"Yes, that was quite an honor. I wear my medals proudly."

"What kind of logs do you want to see?" He asked.

"Your sign-in sheets. We believe three women who attended the seminar were last seen here. We need to verify they came through the Memorial and attended the real estate seminar." Agent Haines stated.

"Look, we have thousands of visitors every year. Even though you know the dates of the seminar, that doesn't mean they visited the Memorial." Geneal Harvey said as he stood up and walked to the file cabinet.

"Yes, we know that. But we're trying to tie down the last place they were at. Most people who attend these seminars also visit the Memorial. Isn't that right?" Jolene asked.

"Yes, most of them come through, but some have seen the exhibit before, and don't come back a second time. The exhibits don't change. They are the same today as they were ten years ago," General Harvey stated.

"We understand that. We're sure the ladies hadn't seen the exhibit before. Do you have the records for that week?" Jolene replied.

"Here are the sign-in sheets for that week you asked for. There is a copy of the day before the seminar and the day after." General Harvey gave the sheets to Jolene.

"Do you have a table? We can go over these?" Agent Haines asked.

"Yes, there is a conference table over there. You're welcome to use it." He pointed to the room next to his office. It had a door, so it would be impossible for him to see exactly what they were looking for or found.

"Thank you, General Harvey. We appreciate your cooperation. We also recommend you don't tell anyone we were here or what we were looking for." Jolene warned.

"Can I ask a question?" General Harvey was showing he was curious.

"Sure." Agent Blay said.

"Why are looking through my records for these persons?"

"They were murdered!" Jolene stated loudly.

"Oh, my goodness. You mean, killed here at the Memorial?"

"We're not sure where they were killed. We're trying to set a timeline." Jolene continued.

Agent Haines took the files, and Agent Blay and Jolene followed.

"Okay, we know who we're looking for." Agent Haines, divide the sheets evenly, and let's start."

They each took a stack and started combing through the names on the sign-in sheets. It was challenging, for they didn't know how they would have signed their names. It was slow going.

After a couple of hours, Jolene spoke up. "Hey, I think I have one!"

Agent Haines and Agent Blay walked around the table and looked at what Jolene found.

"This looks like Sharon Combs's name. The signature of the other two is under hers." Jolene said as she pointed to them.

"Yes, I believe you found them. We need to make a copy of that sheet. Agent Blay takes that sheet and makes a copy. If the general asks what you found, just tell him we found what we were looking for. Nothing else, understand." Agent Haines told him.

"Yes, sir."

"Excuse me, General Harvey, I need to make a copy of this. Do you have a copy machine?" Blay asked.

"Right over there. What did you find?" He asked.

"I can't reveal what it was we found." Blay did as he was told and didn't tell him.

Agent Blay made the copy and returned to the conference room. Agent Haines and Jolene put the file back together as it was when General Harvey handed it to them. He wouldn't know what they found, for everything was the same.

They thanked him and proceeded back to their car. Once inside the car, Agent Haines turned and looked at Jolene.

"What do we do now?" He asked.

"We need to find the hotel register and see if the women checked out." Jolene said.

CHAPTER 11

"Okay, that's our next stop." Agent Haines started the car and drove back to the hotel. As they walked into the hotel, the desk clerk called Agent Haines over and handed him an envelope. He looked at it and then put it in his coat pocket.

Jolene asked the desk clerk if the manager was around?

"He's in the back. Is there something wrong with your rooms?" He said nervously.

"No, we just need to see the manager. You have given excellent service. Don't worry, it isn't about you."

"I'll call him to see if he can see you." The clerk replied.

"Thank you."

"He said to come on back to his office. Go through those doors, and his office is two doors down on the left side."

They followed his instructions and found the manager's office. They walked in and saw him sitting behind a big, oversized desk. His nameplate said Hank Sessoms.

"Hello, Mr. Sessoms. We need to ask you a few questions." Agent Haines told him.

Mr. Sessoms leaned back in his leather chair. He looked at each of them. He wanted to appear unconcerned, but he was nervous, and you could see it in his eyes and facial expressions.

"Mr. Sessoms, we're from the FBI. We need to see your records for the second week of March to the end of March."

"Okay, but we aren't through March yet." He protested.

"If you would let me finish. The year was 2019. We need to see if the three young women were registered here in your hotel." Jolene stated.

"Oh, I see." Sweat was beading up on his forehead.

"I'm afraid I don't have those records." He replied.

"Oh, where are they?" Agent Blay asked.

"They are currently being recorded on the computer. We're going digital, and everything from ten years back is being manually logged into the computer's mainframe. The hotel owners wanted everything to be more efficient and put on this monster of a computer."

"That's fine, but where are your files right now?" Agent Haines asked. He didn't have time for his dribble.

"All the files are at the computer lab."

"Okay, where is the computer lab?" Jolene asked.

"I'll have to show you. Besides, he is under the strictest orders to keep anyone out while working. So, he won't let you in without me telling him it's okay."

"Let's go." Agent Haines spoke softly.

It took about five minutes to reach an old warehouse. It looked like it would fall down in a strong wind.

"You mean you have a computer guy setup inside there?" Agent Blay remarked.

"Yes, that's where they said to set him up. It's quiet, and nobody would suspect someone working in there. You need to blow your horn twice and then once long."

The agents looked at each other! This was playing cloak and dagger stuff. Agent Haines wanted to laugh. Jolene was smiling and holding her tongue.

Agent Haines knew what she was thinking! This was like a military secret mission!

They parked the car after they gave the secret signal. They saw the vast door open and a man standing there. He was grossly underweight and had glasses as thick as Coke bottle bottoms!

"Oh, it's you, Mr. Sessoms. I didn't know who was blowing the secret signal. Is something wrong?" He asked.

"No, nothing is wrong. These are FBI Agents, and they need to see some of our records from five years ago. You have all of those records here. Maybe you can help them find what they are looking for." Mr. Sessoms told him.

"Hello, my name is Benjy. What are you looking for in particular?

"I'm Agent Johnson, and this is Agent Haines and Agent Blay." Jolene introduced them to him.

"Hello, glad to meet you." He replied.

"We're looking for the registration of three women back in March 2017." Agent Haines asked.

"Do you have their last name? I just put in the first six months of 2017. If they were registered, then their names should come up." He replied.

"I didn't realize you were that far along, Benjy." Mr. Sessoms commented.

"Yes, things are going smoothly, sir."

"The first one we're looking for is Sharon Combs."

Benjy jumped to the keyboard. He typed in the name and waited for the response.

It only took a couple of minutes, and her name popped up.

"Sir, here it is. They checked in on the fifth of March, and two others checked in with her. The other two were Judy Mida and Ann Fletcher."

"What day did they check out?" Jolene asked.

"That's just it; they never checked out. Did you know that Mr. Sessoms?" Benjy asked.

"What do you mean, they never checked out?"

"Sir, they still have an open bill going on. It's really high!"

"Please cancel that account!"

"Okay, sir, I'll check them out right away," Benjy replied.

"Mr. Sessoms, that means you have their luggage. Where would you have put it?" Jolene asked.

"I guess they would have put it in the basement. I don't know, honest. The housekeeping department would have taken care of it."

"Benjy, I need a printout of that page. Can you do that?" Jolene asked.

"Of course I can. Do you want the name of the maid who handled their rooms?"

"Yes, please print it out as well." Jolene said.

After they had the printout, they told Mr. Sessoms they would take him back to the hotel. They also wanted to talk to the maid.

"Mr. Haines, I'm not sure if she's working today or not. We'll have to check with her supervisor."

They drove back to the hotel in silence. Mr. Sessoms figured he was in deep, hot water. They had billing for the three women for the rooms. He needed to be uninformed of the billing going to the realtor's office.

When they returned to the hotel, he went straight to his office. He called the billing company and checked on what they were billing.

"Sessoms over at the hotel; I want to speak to someone doing the billing to Maiden Realty."

"Why is there something wrong with the billing, sir?"

"What type of billing do you send to them?" Mr. Sessoms asked.

"They are under contract. We bill the company once a month, and it's paid automatically."

"For the past five years?" He asked.

"Yes, I believe that's where we are."

"Stop billing them now!" He shouted into the phone.

"But sir, they are still at the hotel according to my print outs."

"I don't care what your printout says! They last came here five years ago! You are going to have to find out how much we have to pay back to Maiden Realtor!"

"Yes, sir right away. I'll let you know."

Agent Haines and Jolene just shook their heads. Agent Blay wanted to comment but just stood there with his arms folded.

"Sorry to keep you waiting. I did not know this was going on, honest. I'll check and see if the maid is working."

Mr. Sessoms picked up the phone and called the housekeeping department. "Mrs. Smith, do you know if Mary Busey is working today?"

"Yes, she is, but she has already finished for the day and has gone home. She'll be back tomorrow at six."

"Thank you. Please leave a note for Miss Busey that I would like to meet with her as soon as possible when Miss Busey comes in."

"Is there something wrong, is a guest complaining about her?"

"No, I just need to ask her some questions."

"Alright, I'll leave her a note in her locker."

"Thank you."

"Look, I know you three are registered here at the hotel. It's on the house. The maid will be here at six in the morning. I'm so sorry this all happened. You are my guess at the hotel for your entire stay, food, drink, and anything else you need."

They turned and walked away. Jolene knew what was on Blay's mind. Everything was free. Let's eat!

Jolene looked at Agent Haines. "What do you want?" He asked.

"I believe you have something in your jacket pocket you haven't looked at yet."

"Oh, you know I forgot all about it. Let's go up to the room and we'll see who our fan club has asked us to do." Agent Haines said.

"Oh, wait a minute." Agent Haines walked up to the desk clerk. "Who brought this letter to you to give to me?"

"I don't know, sir. It was one of the neighborhood children brought it in. He said some man gave it to him and a quarter. He was instructed to give it to you personally, but you weren't here, so he left it with me to give to you."

They walked into the dining room and were treated like royalty! The hostess sat them at the best table in the house. The waiter brought over a bottle of champagne. Agent Haines looked at him and wanted to ask, but didn't say a word.

"The house special is a filet mignon with backed potato and a lovely toss salad. I highly recommend it and for dessert, we have a strawberry souffle."

Agent Blay's mouth was watering! Jolene could tell he was ready to dive in before it even got there. They all ordered the special. The waiter popped the cork on the champagne. He poured their glasses, then walked away to put their order in.

"Agent Haines, isn't this kind of unusual?" Jolene asked.

"I would say so! But the manager is probably worried we're going to turn the hotel in for fraud!"

"We could do that?" Agent Blay asked.

"Okay, let's just enjoy it for tonight." Jolene stated.

"I agree. When does the FBI get treated like this?" Agent Blay asked.

"Never my son!" Agent Haines told him.

"Okay, after dinner, we need to regroup and see where we are going next. I guess it determines what we find in the luggage the girls left. If it's still here. The maid might have removed it and sold the items left in them." Jolene stated.

"Yes, that is a possibility, but we have to see what the maid says when she comes in. It might be she's honest and just in the rush of things put the luggage in the ceiler without thinking. People are always leaving things behind," Agent Haines commented.

"Oh, that reminds me, what is inside your coat pocket?" Jolene asked.

"I guess I better look at it before you have a heart attack!" Agent Haines looked at Jolene. He pulled the envelope out of his coat pocket.

He was sitting across the table from Jolene and as he read the note; he looked at Jolene twice and then back down at the note. Jolene wanted to reach across the table and take it from him, but knew better.

"I'll be right back," Agent Haines announced. He got up and left the table and walked into the around the front desk.

He had his cell phone in his hand, dialing a number. Jolene spotted him from the corner of her eye. "Who could he be calling?" She asked.

"What are you talking about?" Agent Blay asked.

"Our boss. He's calling someone. Whatever was on that note must have been really important. But what I can't figure out is why didn't he share." Jolene told Agent Blay.

"I can go out there and ask him?"

"No, just keep quiet. He'll tell us when he's ready." Jolene came back with.

"Hello chief?

"Hello, Agent Haines. Is something wrong?" His voice concerned something had happened to Jolene.

"Look Chief, Jolene doesn't know I'm calling you. We have to figure a way to get Jolene home. I just got a note threating her, listen she doesn't know and I will not tell her."

"Oh my God! What do you mean someone has threatened her life?"

"Yes, that's what I'm saying. If I tell her, you know how she is and she'll be determined to find out who and put him on the ground. Jolene won't give up, you know that."

"Agent Haines, I can't tell you what to do, and I know my daughter. I want her to be safe, but I think she may know and it's your call. You know she will not back down from a threat!"

"Yes, I know. I just wanted to run it by you before I made a rash decision."

"Okay, so you'll tell her, right?" Chief asked with concern in his voice.

"I guess I have no choice. I need to go before she gets suspicious. Talk to you later."

They finished their meal in silence. Jolene knew something was up, but didn't want to ask. She figured he'd talk when he was ready. It had to be something important for him to leave the table so abruptly. Once they had their dessert and coffee, he looked at Jolene intensely.

"Jolene, we need to talk. Let's go to your room." He said to her.

"Alright, what is this about?" She asked.

"I'll tell you when we get to your room." Agent Haines told her.

"Hey, Jolene and I were going to go for a walk around the park! Why need to talk to just her and not me?" Agent Blay asked.

"This concerns Jolene, only you can't go for a walk right now!" Agent Haines snapped.

"Okay, I didn't mean to pry!" Agent Blay replied.

Jolene suddenly became nervous. They always told everything to everyone. Now he just wanted to talk to me? This was concerning to her.

They left Agent Blay in the lobby and headed for Jolene's room. He watched them as they entered the elevator. His feeling was hurt, but he didn't want Jolene to know. He knew she would tell him or Agent Haines once he talked to her.

Once they reached her room, she unlocked the door, and they entered. Jolene turned and looked at him, wondering what was so important that he couldn't talk to Agent Blay at the same time as her. She wondered if it had to do with her father?

"Okay, we're here, what's going on?" Jolene asked with her arms folded in front of herself.

"Jolene, I don't want you to be upset, but I think you should know the note I received was about you." Agent Haines said in a calm voice. He didn't want her to panic.

Agent Haines handed her the note he had received. Jolene opened it and began reading.

'Hello FBI agent; you don't know me, but the lady with you needs to back off this case,

Heed my warning!"

"If she doesn't, she might end up like the dead women you are trying to solve. Go home to FBI agents and leave this case alone! This is the only warning you will receive. Pack up your car and leave tonight! I'll be watching!"

Jolene couldn't believe what she was reading. She sat down on the bed and the note fell to the floor. She looked up at Agent Haines and wanted to say something, but no words came out of her mouth.

"Jolene, I called your father and asked him if I should send you home. He told me to use my judgement. I know you have been shot and have been impaled with an arrow. This was a direct threat to you and to us." Agent Haines didn't know what else to say.

"Sir, you must think this threat was real or you wouldn't have called my father. What did he say?"

"He told me to use my judgement what to do. Jolene you are too valuable to lose and I can't make that decision. You are going to have to make a choice. I'm ready to pack the car and leave here tonight. But this investigation isn't over until we solve it. You are the important part of this investigation. We wouldn't be as far along without you."

"I know dad knows how stubborn I am, and I know he knows you will protect me the best of your ability. If I was any other agent, we wouldn't be having this conversation. I have to know we're getting close to the truth." Jolene said.

"Okay, then you will continue this investigation. Am I right?"

"By all means. We'll have to be more careful of our surroundings and the people we talk with. But yes, I will not be bullied off this case."

"Jolene, do you have your gun with you?"

"Yes sir, always near me."

"I want you to use your holster and wear it on your hip. I'm going to tell Blay to do the same thing."

"I gather you haven't told him about this yet?" Jolene asked.

"No, he doesn't know any of this. I wanted to talk to you first before I set off alarms. You know he cares for you a lot. He's the type to panic before knowing the facts."

"Yes, how well I know. So how are we going to handle this?" Jolene had gained her composure now and was ready to fight.

"I think we should do what the note has suggested. We won't really back off, but we'll make him think we have. So, pack your suitcase and I'm going to get Agent Blay. I'll tell him we have a lead we're following up on have to leave tonight. He'll believe it and we won't have to tell him anything about the note."

"I'll pack my suitcase now. Call me when you are ready to leave." Jolene stated.

"Okay, I have to get Blay up here and tell him we're leaving. I know he's going to protest, so he'll probably call you to see what's going on. Just tell him we have a new lead and have to go to the next town right away before the suspected gets away."

"I can do that. He'll believe me. Sir, what do we do about the women's luggage?" Jolene told him with a half -smile on her face.

"We'll have to figure something out about it. I can call the manager in the morning and tell him we'll pick it up in a day or two. We'll also tell him to be sure to lock it up somewhere. We definitely don't want it to disappear."

Agent Haines call Blay's cell phone and told him to come to the room. Blay started complaining right away before he even reached the room.

"What's going on? You two just left me alone and never told me anything. Jolene and I were going for a walk and now you want me to come to the room! What's going on?" Blay grumbled.

"Just come to the room and I'll explain everything to you," Agent Haines told him.

Naturally, he called Jolene to see if he could get her to tell him what was happening. Jolene did as she said she would. Told him nothing, but he needed to get to his room. Agent Haines would explain everything to him.

Agent Blay was angry he hadn't been included in the talk with Jolene and really wanted to lash out at Agent Haines. Haines was the superior and knew that would only get him into trouble, so he did as he was told. He thought Jolene would tell him, but he was mistaken. He'd have to see what Agent Haines told him.

Agent Blay knocked on Agent Haines door and waited for him to open it. The first thing Agent Haines told him was to sit down. Now his curiosity was really running wild.

"Look, I need you to pack your bag. We're leaving here tonight. I can't have you asking a bunch of questions either. You will just have to trust Jolene and myself. We have a hot lead we need to jump on, so we're moving to another town tonight."

"Okay boss, I get it, but why couldn't I have been in on the conversation with Jolene?"

"Because I didn't need you asking a bunch of questions. We needed to make a quick decision, and I knew Jolene and I could come to an agreement right away with no second guessing." Agent Haines told him.

"Oh." was all Agent Blay had to say. He left to pack his bag so he'd be ready to leave.

Meanwhile, Agent Haines called down to the front desk and wanted to speak to the hotel manager. He never left the hotel until around eleven, so he knew he'd still be there.

"Hello, Mr. Sessoms, this is Agent Haines. We have to leave tonight, but I need you to do something. I need you to move the women's luggage to a safe place where nobody can get access to it. Can you do that?"

"Yes, sir, but I won't be able to do it until I speak with Ms. Busey. She knows where she put she put it, I hope. But yes, I'll see that it is moved to a safe place. Do you know when you'll be back to pick it up?"

"No, sir, but I'll call you when we're on our way back to pick it up. Agent Haines said.

"Very well then, now remember you have carte blanche when you return, sir," Mr. Sessoms responded "Thank you, we appreciate it." Agent Haines replied and hung up.

Agent Haines called Jolene and Blay to see if they were ready to leave. They both told him they would meet him in the lobby.

Mr. Sessoms was waiting for Ms. Busey to arrive at work. It was six-thirty in the morning, and he was pacing back and forth in his office. He called the front desk clerk four times to see if she had arrived. Each time, the answer was the same. At seven fifteen, the desk clerk called Mr. Sessoms and told him she had arrived. He demanded he tell her to report to his office at once.

Ms. Busey did not know what she had done. She had always reported to work on time, and all the guests assigned to her always gave her great compliments about her service. She became very nervous. Her Uniform, green with a white apron, was also shaking. Her white shoes seem to squeak when she walked. They were perfectly white.

She knocked on the door to his office. Ms. Busey heard him say, come in. Slowly, she cracked the door and looked inside. Her boss, the head of housekeeping, was sitting opposite Mr. Sessoms' desk.

"Ms. Busey, we have some questions to ask you, and we want the truth. Do you understand? "Mr. Sessoms asked. There never had been any comments from her assigned floors. Only compliments from the guest she took care of.

"Yes, sir." She replied.

"There were three FBI agents here, and they found out there were three women registered here, and they never checked out for over five years! Do you hear what I'm saying to you?" Mr. Sessoms was nearly screaming at her.

"But Sir, what three women?" Ms. Busey asked.

"They were in 206, 207, 208. Those were your rooms. Why did you not report them as being missing or they had checked out?" The manager of the housekeeping asked.

"But, ma'am, I don't know what you are talking about. I report all checkouts to the desk clerk. He saw me put the keys on the checkout board."

"Well, you sure didn't report these to the desk clerk. This happened five years ago, and we still have them registered at this hotel!" Mr. Sessoms was showing his anger.

"You say this was five years ago? I think I can explain what happened. This was the time of the big real estate seminar, right?" Ms. Busey asked.

"Yes, go on." Mrs. King, the housekeeping manager, asked.

"Their rooms hadn't been slept in for about four days; nothing had been touched. I called down to the desk clerk, and he said to pack everything up and put it in the basement, the lost and found department. We had another group coming in, so I did what he said and put the keys back on the board with the empty room keys. I told Eddie, the desk clerk, that I put the keys back, and he said he needed those rooms. He told me to make sure they were ready for a new guest."

"So, he was aware of those rooms were empty. I hung the keys on the board." Mr. Sessoms asked.

"I don't know, sir; I just did what he told me to do. We have guess leave things all the time. This wouldn't be the first time a guest left their luggage."

"I need you to show me exactly what you did with their luggage." Mr. Sessoms demanded.

Mr. Sessoms and Ms. King followed Ms. Busey to the cellar. They both looked around in awe. They had never seen so much clutter! There were suitcases and plastic bags of clothes all piled on top of each other.

"Oh, my goodness! How long has this been going on?" He asked.

"I do not know. The maids find these things all the time." Ms. Busey Commented.

"Why weren't we notified about all of this?" Ms. King asked.

"Because every time we try to say something to you about this, you tell us to do whatever we need to do. So, they do just that."

"We have to fix this and right away. Did the others label these things?" Mr. Sessoms asked.

"Most of the time. We put their name and their room number on it. If they ask for a missing item, we can find it quicker. Most of them never come back for it."

"Okay, let's get these three pieces over to the lockup building. The FBI is going to come back for them."

CHAPTER 12

Saratoga Springs was just thirty-eight miles from Bolton Springs, New York. Jolene looked it up on the map, and they went there. There would be plenty of motels to check into, and they could quickly drive back to Bolton in less than a half hour. They would need to get the three girls' luggage. They wanted to see what they had left.

They had no trouble finding a pleasant hotel to register. Agent Blay still didn't know what was happening, but knew something was wrong. Jolene was jumpy and was now wearing her gun on her side. Agent Haines was, too. He had told Agent Blay to strap on his as well. He wanted to know why, but Agent Haines told him it was just cautionary. This was hard for him to accept. He wanted to ask questions but feared making Jolene or Agent Angry with him.

Two days passed, and Agent Haines decided it was time to return to Bolton Springs to retrieve the luggage. It might hold a clue who took these women. Maybe even a sample from the skin of the killer. It was worth a try.

The next morning would be perfect for them to return. He would call Mr. Sessoms to let him know they were on their way. He wanted him to be available when they arrived to take them to the area where he had locked up the luggage.

When they arrived, they had the desk clerk to call Mr. Sessoms' office and tell him they were there. Agent Haines didn't want any excuses from him. He had made sure he knew they were coming.

There wouldn't be any excuses he could use. The desk clerk dialed the number and handed Agent Haines the telephone.

"Hello Mr. Sessoms, we're here to collect the luggage left by the three women. I trust you have it locked up like I told you?" Agent Haines asked.

"Yes, sir, just like you said. I'll take you to it. I certainly didn't know it was here, nor did I know the ladies had gone missing." Mr. Sessoms rambled on.

"Relax Mr. Sessoms, we're here only to pick up the luggage. Nothing else, understand?" Agent Haines told him.

He led them to the basement and to a locked room there. He scrambled in his pockets for the key to unlock the door. Once he unlocked the door, he spun back toward the stairs to the first floor. He didn't want any part of those suitcases.

Jolene and Agent Blay carried the cases to the car. They were going to open them there, but took them back to Saratoga Springs. Agent Haines felt it would be more secure. Once they arrived back at the motel, Jolene couldn't wait. Unfortunately, the suitcases were locked!

They placed the cases in the car's trunk. Agent Haines was eager to open them up as well. He couldn't believe they had left everything behind. Whoever took them should have taken the luggage with the girls. This was amazing, for if he knew they were registered there, they would have luggage.

When they arrived back at their hotel, they took the luggage into Agent Haines room. He tried to open the case, but found it locked up.

"Jolene, do you have a hairpin or paper clip?" Agent Haines asked.

"Yes, here's one." She handed him a paperclip.

It only took a couple of seconds for him to open all three suitcases. They were neatly packed. The maid, most, has taken care of putting their items in the suitcases. Jolene started going through each case one at a time. What puzzled Jolene was how the cases got locked, and if the maid locked them, why didn't she give the key to the desk clerk or Mr. Sessoms?

The suitcases were labeled with their names on the handles so they knew whose case they were looking through. It could have been more uneventful. Each contained basic things like a toothbrush, comb, and makeup, and one had a hair dryer. Nothing earth-shattering. The bride's suitcase had several notes she had taken for the upcoming wedding. There was also a diary leading up to the special day to come. The other two the bridesmaids had a diary as well.

Agent Haines looked at Jolene and pointed to an object sticking out of the side pocket of the case. Carefully, with her gloves on, she tried to unzip the pocket, but it was jammed.

"Jolene, we need a pair of pliers."

"Let me look in my bag of tricks." Jolene stated. She pulled her briefcase out; inside, she had pliers and screwdrivers.

"Here, let me do that." Agent Blay took the pliers from her.

He put the pliers on the zipper and pulled on it. It wasn't budging. It would rip if he tried to pull on it any harder. They had to keep everything intact.

"Jolene, do you have any suggestion?"

"Well, we could put soap on it to see if that will make it move. I'm sure whatever is caught in the zipper is keeping it from budgeting." Agent Haines commented.

"Let's try the soap first before we get stupid." Jolene said as she walked to the bathroom to get the soap.

She rubbed the soap up and down the zipper. Slowly, Agent Blay tried to move the zipper. Slowly, the zipper moved. He continued to move the zipper back and forth until it finally unzipped. The paper holding the zipper also had a piece of fabric on it.

"Jolene, can you read the paper?" Agent Haines asked.

"I can read part of it; it says your friends are in trouble, and you must come right away to—. That's all I could read. There is more, but I don't have the stuff to pull it out."

"Okay, let's get it off to headquarters. We need to run the prints off of it as well." Agent Haines told her.

"Elliot put it in one of those plastic evidence bags, and we can overnight it to the agency," Jolene told him.

"Blay, while Jolene and I are gone, can you catalog all the items in each bag? There is probably their address, and maybe their family's address, too." Agent Haines told him.

"Why can't Jolene do all of that?" Agent Blay Grumbled.

"Because I asked you to do it. I also think you are more than responsible for keeping these bags safe. It wouldn't surprise me if someone didn't steal them back if they find out we have them. It wouldn't surprise me one bit. They will know before five o'clock today." Agent Haines stated.

When you put it that way. I understand now. I wouldn't have thought someone would try to steal them. Why, they've been in the cellar for over five years." Agent Blay stated.

"Jolene and I are going to the FedEx Office here in town if we can find one. The cell phone states there is one on Main Street. We should get there just before it closes."

Jolene and Agent Haines started toward his car, parked across the parking lot. All the spaces near the building were taken. Neither of them had an umbrella, so both plummeted with the rain.

Near of them wrote the name the suite cases belonged to. They kind of looked at each other and Jolene laughed, for she knew exactly what he was thinking. She could call Agent Blay and ask him, but that would be something Agent Haines and Agent Johnson would never live down. He'd be using it for a long time against them.

"Whose case was this in?" Agent Haines asked.

"You know, I know how to get it over, Agent Blay. I can call him and tell him to make sure he looks inside all the pockets of the other two cases. Then I'll ask him to look inside of the one we got the paper from. He'll say the name out load to make sure that is the case we're talking about.

"Ann Fletcher's suite case." Agent Blay replied.

"Yes, that's the one we took the paper from." Jolene stated.

"Do you want me to list the paper and what it said?" Agent Blay asked.

"Yes, list this as the note said, okay it's some kind of warning. Apparently. she was told to one girl was in trouble. I can't make out the rest."

"Did you find any prints on the bag?" Agent Haines was eager to see if anyone other than the maid had handled the suite cases.

"We'll Federal Express it back to the home office where they can see if they can raise the writing on it. They have the chemicals to do such a thing." Jolene said.

"Okay, now we have to find a FedEx Office," Agent Haines stated.

"I saw one back aways just as we were going towards Bolton." Agent Blay said.

"Great, this isn't turning into a bad day after all." Jolene stated.

It was a dreary, cloudy day, and the rain coming down in buckets off and on. It was only four-thirty in the afternoon, but it felt like eight or nine o'clock. Jolene didn't like the rain, but because she was with Agent Haines. It makes her feel safe. Just like when she was with her father. This was the perfect time for someone to attack them.

"I'll stay with the case. Sorry, I guess I was being a pain." Agent Blay stated.

They found the FedEx Office and were eager to get this office with them. Once it was in their hands, they felt it was secure. When the home office received the package, they would take care of it right away.

Jolene was first out the door, and Agent Haines followed. Just as they were about to reach the car, a hail of gunfire started! It was aimed directly at them! Jolene and Agent Haines became separated as they tried to find cover from the gunman.

"Agent Haines, are you alright?" Jolene asked.

"Yes, how about you?" He asked,

Then, without warning, a shadow came across the pavement, and Agent Haines was ready. His pistol cocked and aimed at the area he saw the shadow form. They heard sirens coming down the street toward them. Someone must have heard the gunfire and called it into the police.

Jolene fell to the ground as the bullets flew by her head. She lay perfectly still without moving. She could hear footsteps coming closer. Then the footsteps stopped. She couldn't turn her head or move a muscle, so they would think she was dead.

Jolene and Agent Haines were together, hiding behind a car. They couldn't see Jolene, and there wasn't any way to reach her from their location. Agent Blay was upset because he wasn't there to protect Jolene. She wasn't responding to his call-outs over the cell phone!

"Elliot Blay, you know how smart Jolene is. Leave her alone. I'm sure she is okay. Look, if she plays possum and they'll think she's dead, she can get the drop on them. But we have to do our part and keep them in our line of fire."

"I'm sorry, I wasn't thinking. Jolene means the world to me, and when she's in danger, I just can't help myself."

"That's okay, but you have to remember Jolene is an FBI agent, just like me and just like you. We must trust each other to make the right moves and protect our partners. Can you do that?"

"Yes sir! So, what do we do now?"

"You need to get back in the room and keep a sharp eye on that luggage. Someone wants it bad! This gave them the opportunity to get those bags. There has to be something in them. These guys will kill the FBI!"

"Look, I'm going to sneak around the side of the building to get a better look at them. You stay right here where you are. If they start up firing again, the local police are here now!" Agent Haines stated.

"Yes, Sir."

Little did they know Jolene had turned over and caught one of them as he tried to sneak by. She turned him over to the police and told them they would be down to their office to talk to this guy.

Agent Haines and Jolene showed their license and told them where they were staying. Telling the police to hold the guy until they could come down and question him. They wanted to get back to the hotel where they were staying. It feared Agent Blay would be their next hit on their list. They wanted to get those suite cases and couldn't take a chance in Blay losing them.

They drove up to the hotel and turned the light off the car before entering the parking lot. With the lights off, she could see the shadows outside by the yard lights in the parking lot. She saw two men heading for Agent Haines's room.

Jolene called Agent Blay on the cell phone and whispered to him to hide in the closet and wait until they were inside.

Agent Hines had broken three sidewalk lights, so the walkway was dark. He saw the men moving toward his room. He waited until they had opened the door and moved inside. Once they were inside, he presented himself.

"Put your hands up!" He instructed.

"You're covered, so try nothing!" Jolene said as she came behind Agent Haines."

"Boy, I'm glad to see you!" Agent Blay said as he opened the door, hearing Agent Haines voice.

"I bet not as glad as I am to see you!" Agent Haines said as he flipped on the light in the room.

"How many of you guys are there? Are there anymore of you outside in the car?" Jolene asked.

Just then, they heard a van screech out of the parking lot and go toward the main street of Saratoga Springs. Jolene repeated the question.

"That was your ride, wasn't it? It looks like they didn't want to wait around. Who was in that van?" Agent Haines wasn't playing.

"Agent Haines, where is Blay?" Jolene asked.

"I left him out. He headed for the parking lot. We better go get him."

The police surrounded the area where Haines, Blay, and Jolene were staying. They knew they were FBI and almost put the handcuffs on Blay. Jolene pleaded with the police to listen to her, but they just ignored what she was saying.

The Captain of the police department showed up, and he recognized Agent Haines from another photograph he had seen of him.

"Sorry about that, Agent Haines. Are these two with you?" He asked.

"Yes, this is Agent Johnson, and this is Agent Blay. We're here investigating a cold case involving three women killed about five years ago,"

"Oh, I see. I remember something about that case, but it wasn't in our jurisdiction, so we did nothing about it.

"We've heard that twice!" Jolene piped up.

"Agent Haines, what do you want me to do with these guys? Listen, I heard the radio. Apparently, the van flipped over after hiding a boat trailer; he's going to the hospital."

"Can you put a guard on him just in case he isn't hurt that bad and tries to leave?" Agent Haines wanted to question him; as long as he was in the hospital, this was the best place.

"You got it. What about the one we have in custody we took in a little earlier?"

"I'll be down with my partners and we'll question him. If we get nothing, we'll have all three transported to federal lock-up." Agent Haines stated.

He said it before the man they had picked up with the Van. He didn't like the idea of being locked up. There didn't seem to be a choice. He was just as guilty as the other two who tried to shoot the FBI agents.

"Look, my name is Thomas Mat Cows. I don't know what you guys are talking about. I was looking for my cousin. He said he would be there, and I was to pick him up. Honest, that's all."

"So why did you run when you saw the cops show up?" Jolene asked.

"Well, the cops and I don't get along too well. I just wanted to make sure I didn't run into them."

CHAPTER 13

Come on, Mr. Cows. We know you were there with the other two. Don't ignore the fact you were waiting for them. Lock him up." Agent Haines told the officer standing in the room.

"Bring in one of the other guys." Agent Haines ordered.

The guy sat in the chair like it was a recliner. He kept running his fingers through his hair, trying to act cool! Agent Haines knew right away he was playing hardcore and wouldn't be easy to crack!

"What is your name?" Jolene asked.

"I want my lawyer."

"I just asked your name?"

"I get my phone call now!" He demanded.

"Okay, put him back in a cell and have him call his lawyer!" Agent Haines could have been happier. "Bring in the other guy."

"Before you do that, let me try to talk to him." Jolene said in a sexy voice.

Agent Haines motion for her to try.

"Hello, I'm Agent Johnson with the FBI. You can call me Jolene. What is your name?" She asked. She had unbuttoned her shirt a little and told Agent Haines to wait outside and observe for a few minutes.

"My name is Tom Franks."

"Okay, can you tell us why you were shooting at us?"

"That wasn't the plan."

"Tom, tell me what the plan was?"

"Tony and I were supposed to break in and take the suitcases. That's all. Nobody was supposed to get hurt. The guy that hired us said there wouldn't be any problem. Walk in and walk out with the suitcases. Said it would be a piece of cake."

"So, what was your part in this robbery?"

"I was supposed to be the back-up only. Once he came out of the room, I was to make sure nobody was watching them and then signal for the Van to pick him up. We were going to take them to an old condo downtown. The man said he'd pay each of us one hundred dollars."

"Do you know what the man's name is?" Jolene asked.

"No, I'd never met him. It was something like Harry Tower or Cowder, something like that."

Jolene stood up and walked out of the room. Going over to one detective, she handed him a piece of paper with their names.

"Can you run these through the system and see what comes up."

"I think we should run them through the FBI files also. One of them seems to be familiar. I'm sure those guns had to be stolen. That Van was probably stolen as well." Agent Blay said.

"Agent Blay has the FBI run Harry Bower. I think that was the guy who hired these bozos. He's always into something and this sounds like one of his schemes. Take the luggage and then sell it to the parents of the victims. He plays the part of carrying and wanted to help them. He doesn't know who the victims are so he must have a connection to someone in the department who let it slip out."

"But how does he get away with it?" Agent Blay asked.

"He takes his time and follows everyone until he gets something worth taking back to the family. He knows they will pay a handsome sum to get their family's possessions back."

Thirty minutes later, the computers in the police station came back on all three. Most of their crimes were misdemeanors, car theft, breaking and entering. None of them had completed any time in jail or prison.

Jolene wanted to know more about these clowns. From their arrest record, the only one who didn't belong in this threesome was Thomas Cows. It was apparent he had fallen in with bad influences in his name, and now was the time to scare him straight. He was the only one they still needed to lock up. The other two they had placed in the cells.

Jolene talked to them again. Entering the interrogation room. She had all three put in the same room. She had a handful of papers just to scare him.

"Tom? Can I call you Tom?"

"Yes, I don't mind." He replied.

"Good, just so we understand each other, Tom, I want to be honest with you, it doesn't look good for you and your friends," Jolene told him while looking through the papers she had in her hand.

"What do you mean?" Mr. Cows sweat.

"Well, there's the charge of pulling and firing a firearm upon FBI agents, plus none of you have a license to carry a firearm. Breaking and entering to steal evidence in a murder case, then there is also the possibility one or all of you killed these three women. Depending on the charge the district attorney puts on you, you are looking at a minimum of thirty years. Now do you understand Tom?" Jolene said with a serious look on her face.

"Look, Ms. FBI, I knew nothing; I was only supposed to drop them off and pick them back up. Honest, I knew nothing about what they were supposed to do!" Tom was nearly crying when he spoke. Jolene stepped out of the room and the police officer take the others out of the room.

"Leave Tom at the table." Agent Haines told him.

"Well, Tom, I'll see what I can do, but you have to help us to." Jolene said.

"Anything, just tell me what it is you want me to do." Tom answered.

"We're going to put you in the cell next to your two buddies here. We're going to record everything they say. So, I need you to get him to talk about what they were supposed to do with the luggage and where you were supposed to take them with it. Understand the importance of this?"

"Yes ma'am. I'll get him to tell me. What if he asks me why I'm asking so many questions? What do I tell him?"

"Tell them if you are going to get jailed, you want to know why so you can decide whether it was worth it." Tom said with a straight face.

"Yes, that'll be fine. Just remember, this is to help you stay out of jail!" Jolene and Agent Haines spoke up.

"They can't get to me, right?" Tom was very nervous.

"No, they can't get near you. They are separated into their own cells. You'll be safe. Besides, a guard is sitting down there at the entrance. The first sign of trouble, he signals for reinforcements and will have has an army down there."

"How am I going to get the information to you?" He asked.

"We're going to move the two of them. The way we're moving them is one at a time. We'll save you for last. That way, they won't know anything is up." Jolene told him.

"Agent Haines, I think we should head back to home base. We're close to headquarters and we can go from there once we get a few more answers. What do you think?" Jolene asked.

Agent Haines knew something was bothering Jolene but couldn't put his figure on it. He knew she had already put the scenario into what might have occurred. The paper they sent to the lab she was hoping for the last clue.

"Jolene, I think that would be a great idea. This will give us time to put the pieces together and see where we need to go. Meanwhile, Elliot can pretend he's working on the case while eating pizza!" Agent Haines laughed.

"Come on, don't pick on my guy! He hasn't mentioned food once today, and look, it's nearly eight o'clock in the evening!" Jolene said as she patted Blay on the shoulder.

"Look, it's been a stressful day! Can't we just leave it at that?" Agent Blay said.

"Okay, we're all in agreement. We'll return to the hotel, pack up our stuff, and head back to FBI Central. After we check in at our office, we'll drop you off at home, Jolene." Agent Haines stated.

"What about the suitcases? We still haven't done an inventory of the articles in the bags. Do you what to drop them off at the FBI headquarters? Maybe they could catalog everything and it'll be done when we come in tomorrow." Jolene asked.

"Great idea Jolene. They will do it tonight, and we'll have the list on my desk in the morning." Agent Haines replied.

"We should have the note completed also in the morning. I'm surprised we couldn't read it. Jolene usually has something in her bag of tricks for just the right occasion. This time, she didn't. That just took me by surprise!" Agent Blay stated.

"Right now, I just want to get home and go to bed. I'm too tired to think about anything else right now," Jolene stated.

"Jolene, we'll be home in about two and a half hours. I'll drop you off first and then Blay and I will check-in at the office. There really isn't any reason you two have to check in. I can do it for you. I guess I'll go home tonight. I'll drive back in the morning and he can drive his car, picking you up on his way. Is that okay?" Agent Haines asked.

"But there isn't any reason for you to drive back to my house in the morning. I can drive my car if he doesn't want to pick me up?" Jolene said.

"Jolene, are you being serious? You know I'd love for you to ride with me," Blay stressed to Jolene.

They had had little time together on this case, and Jolene was always going in a different direction than him. Even Agent Haines had his own theories about this case. They felt they needed more confidence to bring their ideas into the open.

Jolene was quiet on the entire ride back to her place. Even Blay had yet to say a word on the ride. Whatever was going on was affecting the entire team. Jolene chose this case, so it couldn't be anything they did to influence her decision.

It would be good to be home, and it would be good to see her father. He was an anchor in her life, and she often thought about what it would be like if he wasn't. He always gave her confidence and the ability to choose right from wrong; when she needed reassurance, he was there.

Agent Haines pulled into the driveway at Jolene's house. It only took Chief Johnson a minute to hear the car turning in. He flipped on the porch light so they could see how to get into the house. What he needed to know was it was only Jolene coming in.

Once in the house, Chief looked at her as she sat looking at her board and everything she had added. She knew from her father's eyes he wanted to know she was alright.

"Jolene, are you alright?" He asked.

"Yes, Dad, I'm alright. I just wanted to get home under your roof! Dad, I know there has to be something that sucked these girls in, and they fell for it! That makes me doubly angry for everyone, male or female, have to realize there are bad people out there and they don't! They keep falling for the scams, and other bamboozle tricks people can think of!"

"Jolene, calm down; I've never seen you so uptight. Usually, you get angry, and an hour later, you're laughing." Chief Johnson tried to comfort his daughter, but it wasn't working.

"Dad, we got the girl's suitcases and were about to inventory the contents. We found a note and a piece of fabric in the zipper. When we got it open, I could only read part of the note.

We sent it to the lab here to see if they can make out the letters in the note. It appeared as a man's handwriting but I'm not sure."

"But you were able to read part of the note?" Chief asked.

"Yes, I read part of it and I can imagine what the rest of the note said."

"Okay, let's start from there." Chief said.

"The part of the note which was readable said; 'Your friend is in trouble and is going to need your help. You—', that's all I could read."

"So, what do you think the rest of the note said?"

"I believe it could have said, your friend are in trouble and you need to help her. I'm going to send a car for her in the morning." Jolene elaborated.

"That's a good assumption. Now go a little farther. How was the note delivered. In person, by courier, was it left at the front desk, or pushed under the door of Agent Haines room?"

"See, Dad! That's why I wanted to come home. I give up on myself without you pushing me hard sometimes." Jolene told him.

CHAPTER 14

"Jolene, you would have thought about these same questions I didn't have to remind you. It was there, but you gave up on yourself before you had the answers." Chief told her.

Jolene started writing all the questions that needed to be answered on the board, and they needed them answered. It would be impossible to get someone to remember how a note was delivered to a guest. This could have been the entire case! This made Jolene fighting angry!

"Listen, let's go to bed, and you'll see things a little differently in the morning. Trust me, you'll have the answers you are looking for." Chief told Jolene.

Chief Johnson and Jolene said good night and kissed each other on the cheek. They both retired for the night. Before they went to bed she turned and gave her father a big hug. He hugged her back and holding her made it possible for him to realize she was okay.

Jolene was exhausted from the trip and the gun battle they had just had. She hadn't told her father about that yet and hoped Agent Haines would leave that part out of the story! She knew once he came over the gun fire would be out in the opened.

The following day, Chief's cell phone was ringing. It was Agent Haines. "Good morning, Chief."

"Good morning, to you also." Chief replied.

"How is Jolene this morning Chief? I know she was a little stressed out after yesterday. Thank goodness nobody was hurt. That was partially due to the quick thinking of Jolene. She always has the answers no matter what situation!" Agent Haines said.

"What happened yesterday?" Chief asked.

"We had some nasty visitors that wanted to take our property from us. It was raining like we were having a monsoon. The parking lot at the motel was quickly filling up with water. These two punks started firing at us while we were at the Fedex office and then they tried to steal the luggage belonging to the girls when they found out Agent Blay wasn't with us they came to the hotel where we were staying"

"So, what happened?" Chief asked.

"Jolene laid down in the parking lot pretending to be dead. They walked right by her to my room and opened the door. As they went in, Blay was hiding in the closet and I came up behind them. We were able to arrest all three. Jolene doesn't think the driver of the Van really didn't know what was going on, and when he heard gunfire, he hightailed it out of there."

"So, I gather you didn't get any information from them about why they wanted to seal the luggage?"

"No, but today we're hoping the note we found will give us some more clues. I think someone put these guys up to sealing the luggage for he was afraid there might be some damning evidence found in one of them." Agent Haines said.

"I think you're right. I believe that's what is wrong with Jolene. She's angry at herself for there were so many questions that needed to be answered and now there wasn't anyone to ask those questions!" Chief told him.

"Tell Jolene I called and I'll meet her at the office. Blay has already left for the office. I thought he was going to call Jolene and see if she wanted to ride with him but I guess he changed his mind." Agent Haines stated.

"Hey, are they alright?" Chief asked.

"Yes, they just haven't had much time to be alone. It must be working on them. Who said, love is Easy?" Agent Haines stated and then laughed a little.

Jolene was in the shower, so she hadn't heard any conversation between Agent Haines and him. This was good, so she could come to Agent Haines or her father when she was ready to talk about it.

Her father was correct. Now that she had slept, she felt better and had some of the answers she was looking for. She hadn't noticed Agent Haines had put all three diaries in her bag. While Jolene unpacked her bag, she found them. She placed them on the table and hoped to read them later. Jolene hoped there was something inside one of them to help get some of the answers she was looking for.

Jolene decided to drive her own car. This would allow her to think about what she had going on in her mind. She now had two suspects to look at carefully. Neither of them really had any medical background. But did they? She had to see more into their past to see if either of them had any medical training.

One other option she hadn't thought about and because they were going to the FBI headquarters, she would be able to get the computer wiz, Ricky, to run a background on the two others she thought might be candidates to see if, by chance, they might be able to find out if they had gone to college and took any courses in medicine.

Jolene beat Agent Haines and Blay to the office. She was glad this gave her a chance to speak to Jerry and Ricky before they arrived.

"Good morning, Jerry. I hope I'm not bothering you but I need you and Ricky to do something for me. But it has to between just the three of us, Agent Haines and Agent Blay can't know about this."

"Jolene this is safe with me. What do you want us to do?" Jerry was all ears. Ricky answered her also.

She took out a piece of paper and wrote the names on it. She handed the paper to them. They looked a little funny.

"After I run them do you want me to bring the report to you?"

"No, keep the reports and I'll pick them up when I leave, okay?"

"Sure, I'll put them on my desk in a folder at the end of my desk." Jerry and Ricky smiled big.

"Hey Jerry, what are you doing taking to my girl?" Agent Blay said.

"No, she was telling about the case. Besides I didn't know she was your girl."

"Well, she is, so keep your hands off, understand?" Agent Blay was dead serious.

"Hey don't I have something to say about this?" Jolene spoke up!

They both looked at Jolene with a question mark in their eyes. She didn't know she was Agent Blay's property!

"Hey you two get in here. We have to go over some facts and see where we are." Agent Haines instructed.

"Yes sir." Jolene replied.

"Jolene, what are your thoughts about this case?"

"Well sir, I think we're on the right trail, but what bothers me is the fact the hotel didn't know the girls were gone. Even if the maid did put the keys back on the pegs as being empty."

"Yes. that bothers me too. If the keys were back on the empty rack, why didn't he ask the question about why were the keys returned as empty rooms. He didn't bother asking about the three rooms, he just rented them out as if he knew they weren't there."

"Yes, I was wondering the same thing. I know they are very busy there. But there weren't any conventions that week, so the hotel would have been basically empty, but he rented out those three rooms as soon as he could. He stated they were slammed and needed those rooms."

'Yes, that's a perfect point, Agent Blay."

"What do you think Jolene?"

"There has to be someone we haven't looked yet?" Agent Haines said.

"Yes, I agree. There are two others we haven't look at yet. The general at the memorial. He was a medical officer and the other one is the guard at the door. He was a little suspicious when we said we were from the FBI. He wanted to know why we wanted to see the general." Agent Blay stated,

"He was just doing his job." Jolene stated.

"Yeah, I don't think he'd know a hammer from a surgical instrument. Look I'm working on a theory." Jolene replied.

"Spill your theory." Agent Haines asked.

"No, not yet. I want to be sure before I tell you anything. It's just a wild guess." Jolene stated.

"But if you think it might help with this investigation then maybe we can help." Agent Haines replied.

"Look you have to trust me."

"Jolene, you know we trust you. But if something about this case you have to let us help." Agent Blay said.

"Look it's almost lunch time. What do you say we break until tomorrow. Jolene you can put this on the board and tomorrow we can go through it. We'll meet tomorrow at your house once you have it put on the board. We can go over everything then, okay?" Agent Haines told them.

"Sounds good to me. Besides as you said, it's already lunch time. We'll all be safe at home."

They were walking out, and the sky was turning black. It looked like it was going to rain any minute. Agent Haines had parked on the street, and Agent Blay parked in the garage near Jolene's car.

Jolene made an excuse she left something inside and had to go back for it. Agent Blay said he'd wait for her to come back. Agent Haines decided he'd wait with Agent Blay.

They heard a round of gunfire going off in the front of the building. The car doing the firing came inside the garage at a high speed and continued firing. Agent Blay pulled his gun and aimed it at the car, but it didn't slow down. Jolene had made her way inside the building.

Agent Blay was trying to hide behind some parked cars, but at the rate the car was moving, he couldn't even get a license plate number, and when he tried to stand up, the bullets went over his head. Jolene called on her cell; an officer needed assistance in the parking garage. By the time help arrived, the van was gone.

They called for an ambulance. They didn't know Agent Haines had taken two rounds in the chest, and Agent Blay had three wounds, two in his left arm and one in his right arm. Jolene was lucky she hadn't been wounded, for she was inside the building and hid behind the concrete wall.

Jolene wasn't able to get any rounds off. She blamed herself for not being able to help either of her partners. Agent Haines was hurt bad, and the ambulance seeing him, loaded him up quickly and took him to the hospital first, and Agent Blay was taken in another ambulance.

One of the other agents wanted to take Jolene to the hospital. Her car was riddled with bullets and wasn't drivable. She was going to have to call her father, and that wasn't going to be easy.

Jolene knew there was going to be an investigation. How was she going to tell her father about this?

The bride to be, her boyfriend, Herald Tomas, was the man Sharon would marry. He had been following them for a long time. When they checked him out, his story checked out. There wasn't anything in his background that said anything different.

Jolene's cell phone rang every five minutes. But she knew not to answer it. She was scared to answer it. She turned it off. Thinking it might be the shooter. She wanted to call her father but was too scared to, just in case they had a lock on her phone to trace her position.

CHAPTER 15

The Director of the FBI took Jolene up to his office. She wasn't able to tell him anything about his office. He was hoping she had seen something that would help with the investigation. But she hadn't seen anything.

"I'm going to call your father. I'm going to put you in protect custody for now. There will be two plain clothes FBI agents outside and two inside. Anything you need they will get it for you. Remember you are not to leave for any reason and you are not to go near any windows or step outside. Do you understand Jolene?"

"Yes sir. Do you have an update on the condition of Agent Haines and Agent Blay?"

"No not yet. I do know Agent Haines is still in surgery. Agent Blay is still in surgery also. His surgery wasn't as bad as Agent Haines. Agent Blay will be in the hospital for a couple of days. We'll be moving him to a safe house as soon as he's ready to be discharged. He'll be under protective custody too."

Jolene couldn't help but blame herself for this shooting. She knew they were getting close, and the killer knew it. If they were killed, the investigation would be put on hold. They didn't know Jolene very well. She was more determined now than ever to put his killer behind bars!

The following day, she called the Director on the new cell phone he had given her. Then she called her father. "Hi, Dad. I thought I'd let you know I'm okay. I didn't want you to worry I'm being well protected. They are waiting on me hand and foot."

CHAPTER 16

"Jolene, have you seen the New York Times this morning?" He asked her. "How did they get this so fast? They would have been right there when this happened. Did you see anyone in the area?"

"No, Dad. I'm like being in solitary here. Why, Dad, is there something in I should know?"

"Jolene, it's so good to hear your voice."

"Dad, the number I called you on is blocked by all incoming calls. I can call you, but you can't call me. We should hang up. They said we can only talk for a couple of minutes just in case they could trace the call." Jolene told him.

"Honey, call me whenever you need to. Even if you call and stay on for a minute." Dad said to her.

"Sure Dad. Are you going to work today?" Jolene asked.

"Jolene, do what they tell you to do. Don't be a hero. If you need anything from the house, tell them to bring it to you."

"Yes, Dad, I understand; I'll be alright. I now have three suspects, and I believe I have the right one nailed down. My concern is for Haines and Blay to be alright. The problem is, I need my board, and I know there isn't any way to get it to me!"

"Call me later and we can talk. The Director Said to make our calls short and we have to do what he says." Dad told her.

Jolene and her father hung up. She wanted to say so much more to him, but she knew he was right.

Jolene called the Director. "Sir, you said anything I wanted, you would make sure I got it."

"Yes, that's what I said."

"Well, I need a copy of the New York Times for today."

"Jolene, I rather you didn't see the paper right now."

"Why sir, is there something in it you don't want me to see?" Jolene said in an angry voice.

"Jolene, trust me. It's not a good idea right now."

"Sir, I need to see that paper!"

"Look, I'm your boss, and I believe it isn't the right time."

"I'll have one guard get a copy for you. But you have to promise me you'll call me after you read it, understand?" The Director said to her.

"Yes, sir, I understand. I promise I'll call you after I read."

HEADLINE:

TWO FBI AGENTS SHOT IN THE PARKING GARAGE OF FBI HEADQUARTERS. ONE IN CRITICAL CONDITION AND SURGERY. OTHER ONE SHOT IN BOTH ARMS AND EXPECTED TO LIVE.

New York Times Reporter.

It was the headline on the front page. Jolene was furious! How did they get the story? They were not releasing any information on this. It needed to be made clear who leaked the story to the press. Jolene had an idea and was going to go straight to the Director.

Jolene picked up the phone and call the director. "Look, Director, I know we're keeping this confidential from every one, so how did they get this story?"

"I need three search warrants. Here is a list of the ones I need them for:

Tony Wilson, Guard at the museum; Hank Sessoms, Hotel manager; Harold Tomas, the boyfriend."

"Jolene, why would you need one for the boyfriend? He would be the last of the ones that would want her dead. I can't understand your reason for that one."

"Look, we know the first two would have had firearms experience. The third one, being her boyfriend, may have second thoughts about getting married. If his bride-to-be were to die, the wedding would be off, right? Well, he works for the New York Times; he would have been the first to publish the story, right?"

"Yes, but that still doesn't explain what your reason is for the search warrants." Director wanted an answer.

"We know the first two have weapons training from the positions they held. The Major we know is an avid shooter and always goes to the gun range to keep up his skills."

"That still doesn't explain what you are looking for, Jolene."

"I'm looking for a gun that can rapidly fire by just holding down the trigger. This wasn't just a pistol! If the shooter had been pulling the trigger, he would have been Superman!" Jolene stated.

"Jolene, did you see the car at all?"

"We were parked on the lower deck as you come out the door of the building. I had forgotten something on my desk and turned around to go back and get it. I heard a car coming at a high rate of speed. I turned around to see if it was one agent. I saw a black car speeding in. I moved inside and then heard the gunfire." Jolene stated.

"So, you didn't see the driver at all?"

"No, when I heard the gunfire, I braced myself against the wall and pulled my gun out. He or she was gone in a flash!" Jolene answered.

"So, you didn't see if it was a woman or a man?"

"No, sir."

"Okay, then we also need to look at the bridesmaids." The Director told her.

"I want to wait on that just now. I want to see what weapons these guys have hiding in their closets."

"So, you have doubts about the bridesmaids also?"

"There is one I have doubts about. They both have diaries, but I haven't gone through them yet."

"Let's go with your first thought first, and after that, we can look at the diaries." The Director stated.

"Do you think we can get the warrants?" Jolene asked.

"Well, I don't know. We have to have probable cause to ask for warrants. Once we can match the castings with what kind of gun we're looking for, we might get the D.A. office to issue the search warrants."

"They found plenty of castings at the scene. The lab is working on them now. Whoever it was really was careful. There weren't any fingerprints on any of them." Director stated.

"There has to be something I'm missing!" Jolene said in an angry voice.

"Look, you are very lucky you didn't go up to the hospital. Calm down. Let's put our heads together and see what we can come up with."

"Yes, I know Director."

"By the way, have you called your father?"

"Oh my God, no I haven't! I better call him right away. He gets the New York Times every morning!"

"Yes, I would suggest you call him right now."

"I need to go to the hospital. Can you get someone to take me?" Jolene asked.

"I'll take you. I think we need to assign two agents to protect you for the next few days. We don't know what the motive was in this shooting. We don't know if their aim was to take all three of you out. It's apparent they were after you and your partners. You must be getting close to finding the killer or killers!" The Director added.

"I won't work with anybody but my partner's director. I know it's too much to ask. I have another request."

"You know, that might be a good idea. If the killer thinks we have you off the case, then he'll think he's won."

"I'm going to call my dad."

"Okay Jolene. Don't leave the Director's office. What was it you wanted? You said one more thing?" Her father asked. "Nothing Dad."

"Can you call Ricky up here? Also, the boyfriend he's a report for the times. How did he know about the shooting if we're keeping it under raps?" Jolene asked.

"That's a good question. Whoever printed this story had to be on scene. You need to stay out of sight. They don't know who was shot yet."

"I'll use the inner office space to call my dad, if that's okay?"

"Sure, just close the blinds so he doesn't see you."

"Okay." The Agents who brought her back to the office used the back stairway so nobody would see her come in.

Meanwhile, ballistics called the Director.

"Sir, this is Darlene from the lab. Those casings we ran have a unique mark on them. We've seen it twice before. Several years ago, there was a shooting, and they had the same marking on them. No fingerprints, just this mark on it."

"Thank you, Darlene. Do you have down what case this was involved with?"

"No sir, sorry. I just remember seeing this mark. It was so unusual. It was as if the shooter had marked these bullets by hand." Darlene stated.

"Please write up your report. Also, send a couple of casings up to me. See if you can find the case it was involved with."

"I'll see if they are still in the system. I'll send the information up to you."

"Jolene, I have Ricky coming up. What did you want him to look up for you?"

"Director, have him look up both these men, no all three have him look up their history of what they did when they finished high school. There has to be a record of where they went to college and what the classes they took in college. Whether they finished college or bombed out of the classes, they were taking and chanced three majors."

"Jolene you're grasping at straws!" He told her.

"Yes sir, I know I'm grasping at straws, but there has to be a connection somewhere that I'm missing." Jolene replied.

"Okay, I'll have him look."

"But please don't tell him I'm here. The less everyone knew, the better it is." Jolene told him.

"Yes, I agree. I've told the two agents that guarded you last night have been told the same thing. If anyone asked them if you are still alive, they were told to tell them no comment."

"One of them have already been approached by a report to tell him who was involved in the shotting and if they are still alive or not. The nurses have all been instructed the same thing. In fact, we have given both of the agents' different names so they can't tie them to you. Now call your father. He's going to blow up our switch broad. He's been calling every half hour, wanting to know where you are!"

"Yes sir, I'm calling him right now on the secure line you gave me."

The phone rang several times before he picked up the call. "Hello Chief!"

"Who is this calling?" Was the first words out of his mouth. The line of the Director had given her a secure line which distorted her voice.

"Look, Chief Johnson, this is a person you have been trying to reach all morning. I called you just a little while ago. I would have called you sooner, but I had to wait until they had another secure line for me to use. They said you have been calling every half hour. This is to tell you I'm just the same as when I left."

"Jolene, you don't know how I've been so worried. I wish they had told me you weren't hurt. When I opened the paper this morning and saw those headlines, I fell to my knees and when nobody could tell me anything made me just that more eager to know whether you were okay. Yes, I know you talked to me earlier, but then an awful question came to mind."

"Look, I can't call for a while. We don't know how much these people know about me. They may have your phone tapped. I love you, dad! I'll try to call you later or tomorrow."

"I love you too. Please be safe."

"The Director is making sure of that, dad. Bye for now."

"Jolene, have you seen the New York Times this morning?" He asked her. "How did they get this so fast? They would have been right there when this happened. Did you see anyone in the area?"

"No, Dad. I'm like being in solitary here. Why, Dad, is there something in I should know?"

"Jolene, it's so good to hear your voice."

"Dad, the number I called you on is blocked by all incoming calls. I can call you, but you can't call me. We should hang up. They said we can only talk for a couple of minutes just in case they could trace the call." Jolene told him.

"Honey, call me whenever you need to. Even if you call and stay on for a minute." Dad said to her.

"Sure Dad. Are you going to work today?" Jolene asked.

"Jolene, do what they tell you to do. Don't be a hero. If you need anything from the house, tell them to bring it to you."

"Yes, Dad, I understand; I'll be alright. I now have three suspects, and I believe I have the right one nailed down. My concern is for Haines and Blay to be alright. The problem is, I need my board, and I know there isn't any way to get it to me!"

"Call me later and we can talk. The Director Said to make our calls short and we have to do what he says." Dad told her.

Jolene and her father hung up. She wanted to say so much more to him, but she knew he was right.

Jolene called the Director. "Sir, you said anything I wanted, you would make sure I got it."

"Yes, that's what I said."

"Well, I need a copy of the New York Times for today."

"Jolene, I rather you didn't see the paper right now."

"Why sir, is there something in it you don't want me to see?" Jolene said in an angry voice.

"Jolene, trust me. It's not a good idea right now."

"Sir, I need to see that paper!"

"Look, I'm your boss, and I believe it isn't the right time."

"I'll have one guard get a copy for you. But you have to promise me you'll call me after you read it, understand?" The Director said to her.

"Yes, sir, I understand. I promise I'll call you after I read."

HEADLINE:

TWO FBI AGENTS SHOT IN THE PARKING GARAGE OF FBI HEADQUARTERS. ONE IN CRITICAL CONDITION AND SURGERY. OTHER ONE SHOT IN BOTH ARMS AND EXPECTED TO LIVE.

New York Times Reporter.

It was the headline on the front page. Jolene was furious! How did they get the story? They were not releasing any information on this. It needed to be made clear who leaked the story to the press. Jolene had an idea and was going to go straight to the Director.

Jolene picked up the phone and call the director. "Look, Director, I know we're keeping this confidential from everyone, so how did they get this story?"

"I need three search warrants. Here is a list of the ones I need them for:

Tony Wilson, Guard at the museum; Hank Sessoms, Hotel manager; Harold Tomas, the boyfriend."

"Jolene, why would you need one for the boyfriend? He would be the last of the ones that would want her dead. I can't understand your reason for that one."

"Look, we know the first two would have had firearms experience. The third one, being her boyfriend, may have second thoughts about getting married. If his bride-to-be were to die, the wedding would be off, right? Well, he works for the New York Times; he would have been the first to publish the story, right?"

"Yes, but that still doesn't explain what your reason is for the search warrants." Director wanted an answer.

"We know the first two have weapons training from the positions they held. The Major we know is an avid shooter and always goes to the gun range to keep up his skills."

"That still doesn't explain what you are looking for, Jolene."

"I'm looking for a gun that can rapidly fire by just holding down the trigger. This wasn't just a pistol! If the shooter had been pulling the trigger, he would have been Superman!" Jolene stated.

"Jolene, did you see the car at all?"

"We were parked on the lower deck as you come out the door of the building. I had forgotten something on my desk and turned around to go back and get it. I heard a car coming at a high rate of speed. I turned around to see if it was one of the agents. I saw a black car speeding in. I moved inside and then heard the gun fire." Jolene stated.

"So, you didn't see the driver at all?"

"No, when I heard the gunfire, I braced myself against the wall and pulled my gun out. He or she was gone in a flash!" Jolene answered.

"So, you didn't see if it was a woman or a man?"

"No, sir."

"Okay, then we also need to look at the bridesmaids." The Director told her.

"I want to wait on that just now. I want to see what weapons these guys have hiding in their closets."

"So, you have doubts about the bridesmaids also?"

"There is one I have doubts about. They both have diaries, but I haven't had a chance to go through them yet."

"Let's go with your first thought first, and after that, we can look at the diaries." The Director stated.

"Do you think we can get the warrants?" Jolene asked.

"Well, I don't know. We have to have probable cause to ask for warrants. Once we can match the castings with what kind of gun we're looking for, we might get the D.A. office to issue the search warrants."

"They found plenty of castings at the scene. The lab is working on them now. Whoever it was really was careful. There weren't any fingerprints on any of them." Director stated.

"There has to be something I'm missing!" Jolene said in an angry voice.

"Look, you are very lucky you didn't in up in the hospital. Calm down. Let's put our heads together and see what we can come up with."

"Yes, I know Director."

"By the way, have you called your father?"

CHAPTER 17

"Oh my God, no I haven't! I better call him right away. He gets the New York Times every morning!"

"Yes, I would suggest you call him right now."

"I need to go to the hospital. Can you get someone to take me?" Jolene asked.

"I'll take you. I think we need to assign two agents to protect you for the next few days. We don't know what the motive was in this shooting. We don't know if their aim was to take all three of you out. It's apparent they were after you and your partners. You must be getting close to finding the killer or killers!" The Director added.

"I won't work with anybody but my partner's director. I know it's too much to ask. I have another request."

"You know, that might be a good idea. If the killer thinks we have you off the case, then he'll think he's won."

"I'm going to call my dad."

"Okay Jolene. Don't leave the director's office. What was it you wanted? You said one more thing?" Her father asked. "Nothing Dad."

"Can you call Ricky up here? Also, the boyfriend he's a report for the times. How did he know about the shooting if we're keeping it under raps?" Jolene asked.

"That's a good question. Whoever printed this story had to be on scene. You need to stay out of sight. They don't know who was shot yet."

"I'll use the inner office space to call my dad, if that's okay?"

"Sure, just close the blinds so he doesn't see you."

"Okay." The Agents who brought her back to the office used the back stairway so nobody would see her come in.

Meanwhile, ballistics called the Director.

"Sir, this is Darlene from the lab. Those casings we ran have a unique mark on them. We've seen it twice before. Several years ago, there was a shooting, and they had the same marking on them. No fingerprints, just this mark on it."

"Thank you, Darlene. Do you have down what case this was involved with?"

"No sir, sorry. I just remember seeing this mark. It was so unusual. It was as if the shooter had marked these bullets by hand." Darlene stated.

"Please write up your report. Also, send a couple of casings up to me. See if you can find the case it was involved with."

"I'll see if they are still in the system. I'll send the information up to you."

"Jolene, I have Ricky coming up. What did you want him to look up for you?"

"Director, have him look up both these men, no all three have him look up their history of what they did when they finished high school. There has to be a record of where they went to college and what the classes they took in college. Whether they finished college or bombed out of the classes, they were taking and chanced their majors."

"Jolene you're grasping at straws!" He told her.

"Yes sir, I know I'm grasping at straws, but there has to be a connection somewhere that I'm missing." Jolene replied.

"Okay, I'll have him look."

"But please don't tell him I'm here. The less everyone knows, the better it is." Jolene told him.

"Yes, I agree. I've told the two agents that guarded you last night have been told the same thing. If anyone asks them if you are still alive, they are told to tell them no comment."

"Ricky, I have a special job for you to do. You are not to tell anyone what you are doing and if they ask, you are to tell them you are working on a special project for me, understand?"

"This is for Jolene, isn't it?" He answered back.

"Did I say that?"

"No, sir. Sorry Sir." Ricky started to sake. He had never been to the Directors' office, which made him nervous.

"You are to report back to me with your findings. No one else is to know what you are working on, and if they ask or ask you to do something else for them, you are to tell them nothing except you are working on something for me, understand?"

"Yes, sir."

Ricky went back to his station. He should have remembered to take the names down. The Director wanted him to look up. Now he had to go back to his office and ask him. This was embarrassing for him. He thought about just calling him, but he knew it wouldn't be right. So, he returned to the elevator and pushed the top floor button.

Politely, he knocked on the door of the Director's office and waited to hear him say come in.

"Come in."

"I thought you'd be back! Here are the names of the guys I want you to run. This is from the time they got out of high school to now. Do you understand?"

"Yes, sir."

"First, I want you to run Tony Wilson, second Hank Sessons, and third, Harold Thomas."

"Sir? Isn't Harold Tomas the boyfriend of the girl that was killed?"

"Yes, how do you know that?"

"He's a reporter, and he's been calling here all morning trying to get information about the two agents who were shot yesterday. He told one agent down stairs he had a right to know if it was two males or one female. They didn't tell him anything."

"Are you sure?"

"Yes sir. I was standing at his desk and he told him he couldn't comment on who it was, for it was an ongoing investigation."

"The reporter started yelling at him and the agent hung up on him." Ricky stated.

"What agent was it that took the call?"

"Agent Brice, sir. Everyone down stairs is really upset and has promised that anyone that calls about their condition they are going to hang up on them."

"Good for them. You tell them that's just what I want them to do." The Director said with a semi-smile.

"Yes, sir." Ricky turned around and left the Director's office.

The Director knew Jolene wanted to go to the hospital and check on Agent Haines and Blay. The Director knew it wasn't a good idea to be seen in public. He still had to get Jolene to another safe house and put her in a disguise so nobody would know her. They would take the back elevator so nobody would see them leave. He already had two agents to stay with her while she was protected.

He also knew Jolene was going nowhere once she saw the reports that Ricky was running. It didn't matter to hear if it took all night. She wasn't budging!

It was dark, and a storm was coming up. The sky had turned black, and lightning flashed. Jolene didn't like storms, and this was one of those that would dump a lot of water. She didn't know where they would take her, and she would only have a cell phone to call with. A storm like this would make it impossible for her to reach anyone.

Ricky called the Director's office and told him the computers were down. "Sir, the storm has the computers down. I finished Tony Wilson's report. I can bring it up to up if that is okay?"

"Yes, bring it up. You should come up to my office with the stairs just in case the power goes out."

"Yes, sir." Ricky knew he was right. The power had been going off every few minutes. It was just a matter of time before it went out until the storm was over.

The Director was waiting for him when he arrived. Ricky, knocked on his door and heard him say come in. He walked in, and the Director held out his hand. Ricky put the report in his hand. Jolene was in the secure room, so she couldn't be seen by anyone.

"That's all Ricky. If the power comes back, please continue to run these reports."

Ricky thought to himself, this could take all night! The one he just ran had taken several hours tracking this guy down.

"Yes, sir."

After the Director opened the report. Jolene was in the other room but heard Ricky when he came in. She wanted to make sure he was gone before she came out. The Director called for Jolene to come into his office.

"We have the first report. I'll take the first half and you can take the second half. Is that okay with you?"

"Yes, that's fine with me," Jolene answered.

They both started reading. The power went out completely. His office was equipped with a couple of solar lights, which were charged. They could continue reading the report. Only Wilson graduated high school, and after graduating high school, he entered the army and spent six years in the listed army. He joined the medical core and became an assistant for the surgery team.

After he got out, he entered college to become a medical physician studying surgery. After two years, he was kicked out of the program for being overzealous. Making too many personal choices without considering the patient and what was needed in the patient's treatment.

"Did you see this?" Jolene asked. She handed him the sheet with the information on it.

"Yes, I thought there was something to it. I just read he also won several medals at the gun range for marksmen's ship."

"He was discharged with a dishonorable discharge. The cause of this was he was operating on serviceman, whether they needed it." The Director told Jolene.

"So, he has the guns. I bet hiding in his house or apartment. He probably has the surgical instruments too. See, we need those search warrant for him definitely." Jolene Stated.

"Let's see what the others say first. We want to do all three of them if we're going to search one. Why not all three?" Director stated.

"Have you called the hospital and seen how the guys are?" Jolene asked.

"Agent Blay is doing fine. He has to wear a sling on both arms for a few days."

"Will not release him for about a week. They want to make sure he's healing properly."

"What about Agent Haines?" Jolene was eager to learn."

"Agent Haines is on a ventilator. His surgery was over six hours, and it was very touch and go. He is suspected of making a full recovery. That's the good news."

Jolene had tears running down her cheeks. The toughness she had always shown was suddenly wiped out. The Director put his arms around her. He wanted to comfort her, for he knew what she was thinking.

"Look, Jolene, this wasn't in any way your fault. So don't even go there with this. The FBI faces these challenges daily, which wasn't an exception. We don't know if it was because of another case they had worked on or this one you were working on."

"But, Director, if I had chosen another case that was older, we might not have been in this situation!"

"How do you know that?"

"I don't, but this one was newer than the others we were looking at!"

"Eventually, you would have had to investigation this one. Just get that out of your head right not, understand?" The Director told her.

"Look, Agent Bryant is going to take you to the safe house. And he is going to stay with you till morning. Then Agent Turk will be there in the morning to relieve him. These are the only Agents I'm assigning to you as protection. Keep you gun handy and on your hip. Nobody knows where this safe house is located and they don't know who they are going to be protecting."

"Isn't that going to be a little hard if they don't know who I am?" Jolene asked.

The power came back on. "Jolene, I think you should go. I'll keep the reports here in my office. There is a closet in the safe room with a couple of wigs. Go in there and change your clothes and put on a wig. I'll have Agent Bryant come up and escort you down to a waiting car."

"Why can't I just stay here? Ricky might come up with the next report and I won't be here!" Jolene stated.

"Look Jolene, I'll have Agent Turk bring you back in the morning. Promise me you won't tell them who you are, and you have to dress up like you are going out. That's so they don't recognize you."

"Yes sir, I promise."

Jolene looked through the closet and found several outfits. There was one dress she liked. It was solid black, and the shoes were red, just in her size. She looked for a wig. Her blonde hair had to be covered, but she couldn't see herself in the black wig. There was a long-haired red wig that she tried on. It was perfect. Now, she had to put on makeup. Everything was too extreme for her taste. But he had told her to put it on. This was his order, so she tried to use it like he said.

When she walked out, the Director told her it was perfect! Nobody would recognize her with all this on. Even the inserts to enlargements for her breast in the dress to make her breast larger. She looked like a hooker! Even the other accents would think the Director had ordered a hooker for his entertainment.

Now, this was going to be hard to deal with all day, Jolene thought to herself.

"Director, do I have to keep this on all day?" Jolene asked with a smirk on her face.

"Yes, and don't let anyone see you without this carp on! Do you understand?"

"Yes, sir."

"Take a couple of those dresses with you so you'll have something to change into. Keep the wig and the shoes." The Director told her.

"Yes, sir," Jolene answered.

The Director called for the agent to come to his office. His intention was to provide instructions on what to do with her. His desire for her not to be seen at the hospital persisted. He had called the hospital to get a report on the two agents. He knew Agent Blay was doing okay. Agent Haines was on life support and still wasn't out of danger.

He hadn't told Jolene how serious it was. He didn't want her to know it was touch and go. The doctors hadn't said whether he was going to make it. The Director didn't want Jolene to know the details of his condition. Agent Blay would recognize her voice. The Director didn't want her to see him either, for one word out of her mouth, and he'd know it was Jolene. Agent Blay hadn't been told about Agent Haines, and they were instructed not to tell him anything about his condition.

The only thing that kept him from knowing where they were put was, they had changed their names on the admission forms so nobody would know where they were in the hospital. The newspaper was fishing to find out who had made it during the shooting and asking questions. Nobody would answer them, which made him furious! He tried every way to find out who had been admitted and where they were in the hospital. If he saw this woman going to either of their rooms, he'd know it was Jolene, which would be wrong.

"Director, why can't I see the guys at the hospital?" Jolene asked.

"Jolene, trust me. Not that I don't want you to see them; we have to be careful. You know Agent Blay will recognize your voice, and I know you and him are in a relationship. Agent Haines told me. One word from you, and he'll know it's you! That reporter has been nosing around to find the guys, and if he finds out, well, you know what that would mean."

"Yes, sir, I know you are correct. It's just that I can't see for myself how they are."

"I know Jolene, but I promise I'll let you know if there is any change." The Director told her.

"Okay, I trust you. But you have to tell me if there is any change!" Jolene told him.

"Jolene, I promise you I will. I gave my word." He gave her a hug. "You know I look like a hooker and feel like one too!" They both laughed.

"Thanks Director!" Jolene said and put her smile on.

"Look, I hope the guys protecting me don't get the wrong idea about this decision about you and think I'm having an affair. That would be all I need is for my wife to think I'm having an affair. She'd probably leave me in a heartbeat."

"Director, the guys protecting me won't say a word about your affair!"

They just laughed and looked at each other with cheerful eyes.

The Director called down to the floor where the agents were and told Agent Turk to come to his office. He was ready for her to be moved, so it looked like she had been a guest of the Director.

The storm seemed to pass, and Jolene relaxed a little. Agent Turk didn't know who he was moving but knew it was the Director's orders, so he had to follow them. Jolene found an old bag to put her clothes in.

CHAPTER 18

He arrived shortly after and saw Jolene sitting there in the Director's office. He looked at her and put a smile on his face. The Director looked at him and couldn't help but tell him the woman was a witness to a case in which the FBI was working. He changed her name to Jody Smith. He had forgotten to tell Jolene about her name, so she looked at him with surprise.

Agent Turk put his hand out to shake hers. She had put her gun in the suitcase. So, she looked like just another person. The Director told Agent Turk to take the back stairs to remove Jolene. Because he didn't want anyone to see her.

"Yes sir. Will anyone relieve me?"

"Yes, he'll be around twelve midnight to relieve you. You'll have to come back at twelve noon. You're not to communicate with this person? Do you get it?" The Director Stressed.

"Yes, sir." Agent Turk picked up her bag. They started to the waiting car. Agent Turk had moved his car over to the back stairway so she could get in the car so nobody would see her.

Ricky called Captain's office to tell him he had a report on General Harvey that Jolene had him run. He didn't know what to do with it since he hadn't heard from her. He hadn't known about the report being run on him, so he brought it to his office. Ricky didn't want to cause Jolene any trouble, but he didn't know what she wanted with it.

The Director told him to bring it up to his office. He knew there had to be a reason for it, and he wanted to read the report before he asked Jolene about it. Her instincts were always right on.

Ricky brought him the report. He told him thank you and read it. He had graduated from high school and went to college to become a medical doctor. Taking the three-read program, he did so. He graduated with honors and then joined the army as a medical doctor. He knew Tony Wilson, and they hooked up. They began a surgical unit on the outside of their duties. He was discharged at the same time as the General. Both received a discharge at the same time.

The General became Director of the Memorial, and he ensured Wilson was hired at the same time as a guard at the Memorial. The side work they did involved operating on people who couldn't afford surgery. They did this at night when nobody would know. They made sure they told their patients they couldn't tell anyone who had done the surgery on them, or they would be back and wouldn't be pleased to see them. The fantastic thing about these men was that they went to the same firing range, and both had medals for their shooting ability.

It was documented in the report. They never had enough to take them to court, so no charges were ever filed. Only complaints were made, with no investigation to follow up on the allegations. This was another one she hadn't mentioned to him. He knew she would have. Because there was so much going on, he couldn't be blamed for not telling him.

The odd thing about this was she had three suspects for whom she wanted warrants; now, there would be four for whom she wanted warrants. This would be a probable cause for these all. The instruments would be at their homes. Plus, they would find the guns that could have been used to shoot these agents. The mark on the bullets would be found at one of their houses.

He was still waiting for the ballistics report to show him what other case these markings had been found. Because the power had been off, he knew searching in the dark wouldn't have been easy. The power was back on now, so she could search again.

The Director had to wait for the fourth report to be run. This would be the last of the ones Jolene had told him to run. It was time to see the district attorney about the warrants he needed for the four individuals. He knew they would have questions, but he knew how to sidestep them. Because it was two of the agents, he knew she would be more likely to issue the search warrants, even though they didn't have any objective evidence. It was the Director pushing her buttons and getting on her sympathetic side.

District Attorney Julie Sims will listen, but sitting behind her desk and listening to the Director, she knew he was angry at the shooting of his agents. It was even worse; one was his senior agent and was now on live support.

"Look, Julie, Agent Haines may not come out of this. The doctors said he might have a thirty percent chance of surviving. Agent Haines might not return to work even if he survives. He's one of our best agents. You know that. Look at how many cases he's assisted you in taking to court and helping you win!"

"I know Director. But without the proper evidence, you know there isn't one judge that will sign off on the warrants."

"How is your witness holding up?"

"What witness are you talking about?"

"I suppose it's Jody Smith?"

"Okay, how do you know about my witness? Nobody is supposed to know I have a witness. So, who told you?"

"Will, I know you were trying to be careful, but someone is always around. Anyway, one agent was parking his car and saw a hooker coming down your backstair way. He told my secretary, and she told me. I know you aren't having an affair, so it had to be a witness. Am I correct?"

"Yes, but how did you find out her name?"

"Your Agent Turk told his relief, and he told the clerk in the lab."

"Oh Yeah, it's about a casing we found at the scene. It has a unique marking on it. It was involved in another shooting. I wanted to find the case this was connected to. I need to see if the marking is the same."

"I see. You think whoever shot the agents was involved in another case? Could it be possible this guy is a gun for hire?"

"It could be, but I must find out if the markings match. It might be a case Agent Haines worked on several years ago."

"How has Jolene been holding up since this all happened? You know she has become a genuine celebrity around here."

"Jolene is as tough as nails. She's holding up well. We put a significant dent in those cold cases in the cellar. We were fortunate to recruit her for the FBI."

"Is she working on the case?"

"No, right now, she needed to take some time off. Besides, she doesn't have any partners."

"But can't you assign a couple of agents to her so she can continue?"

"Why? She'd have to bring them up to speed with the case. Not that simple."

"Okay, but without evidence to support warrants, our hands are tied. You know that!" DA Sims said as she walked around her desk and put her hands on his shoulders for reassurance.

"Yes, I know, but the case has been dead for five years. Another few days will not make a difference."

"I supposed, but I really need something to offer the judge. Can you get a hold of Jolene and see if she has anything to go on?"

"I'll speak to her and see if there is anything she can give us. I appreciate your help."

"I know you do. If the lab can get that case file with the marking on it, let me know, so maybe we can tie the two agents shooting to the same guy."

The Director went back to his office. He was eager to see if the file had been found. This was a unique marking, and he was sure nobody else would have used it. It had been engraved on each bullet casing by hand.

His phone was ringing as soon as he walked into his office. He saw it was Ricky calling him.

"Hello, Ricky. Do you have another report for me?"

"Yes sir. This one is very interesting. I'll bring it right up to you."

Ricky knocked on the door and waited for him to say come in.

"Sir, I have the report on that reporter. Harold Tomas, it appears he was engaged before about a year ago. Also, his college days weren't so great! He was expelled three times. Each time, his father paid a pretty good sum to get him back into the college."

"I'll read it. Thank you, Ricky. You still have one more to run, right?"

"Oh, you're talking about Hank Sessons, the hotel manager?" Ricky asked, with a puzzled look on his face.

"Yes, see if you can get it done this morning."

"Yes, sir, I'll do it right now. Sir, can I ask you a question?"

"Okay, what?"

"Could you tell Jolene I've done a good job for you?"

"Yes, I'll let Jolene know. Now get busy and remember, you can't tell anyone what you are working on, got it?"

"Yes, sir."

Ricky went back to his station. He typed in Hank Sesson's name, and the computer began spitting out paper as soon as he did. It started when he was in high school and continues now. The Director would be delighted with his results on this guy.

The Director began reading the report printed out on Harold Tomas. He had been arrested several times for interrupting the police while trying to arrest them. Breaking and entering using his press pass. When he was in college, he had been kicked out of almost every college in New York. As a last straw, his father paid a handsome son to the college to keep him there and see that he graduated. His major was writing. He did very well. This is where he became a reporter for the college press.

Literally, journalism was what he really excelled in. He had also been arrested for abuse by his former girlfriend, whom he had to propose to marry. They broke up after six months before the wedding when he beat her up. She left him and filed charges against him, but his father paid a handsome sum to her to drop the claim.

There was also the fact Jolene had brought up. How did he know two agents had been shot in the garage? No press release or information was given out by anyone.

Jolene paced the floor in the tiny house they had hidden her in. She tried hard to remember what she had seen. The only thing that came to mind was the car racing through the garage. She remembered it was black, but nothing came to mind outside of that.

She picked up the cell the Director had given her and called her father. It rang several times with no answer. This concerned her, for he always answered with a couple of rings. Her next call was to the Director.

"Director, I hate to bother you, but I tried to call my father this morning, and he didn't answer his phone. He always answers within two rings."

"Maybe he was just tied up."

"No, that's not it. Something is wrong. Can you send someone out there and check on him? Please?" Jolene pleaded with him.

"Jolene, is everything else alright?"

"Yes, but I'm going stir crazy out here!"

"Yes, I can imagine. But this is for your protection, and we want nothing to happen to you."

"I need to get home! I need to be working on this case! Nothing is getting done!"

"Yes, I know Jolene, but this is only until we connect to this case or another one. Agent Haines had been working on some time ago."

"So, if this was a case Agent Haines was working on before this one, then I can go home." Jolene said with excitement in her voice.

"I didn't say that. We have to be sure. I'll let you know."

"Did you check with the hospital this morning?"

"Yes, they are both doing better and Agent Blay might go home by the end of the week if he continues to do well."

"What about Agent Haines?"

"They still have him on the machine. The doctor said they may take him off the ventilator by the end of the week as well. He continues to improve."

"Look, just check on my father, please. Can you call the Agent on duty with me so I can call him?"

"Yes, Jolene. I'll call him to tell you to call me first."

"Can I come in to the office for the day?" Jolene was still pleading with him. She could feel the walls closing in on her in the cabin they had her in. The sky was clear and she could tell it was going to be a sunny day. If only she could go for a walk would help her deal with this isolation.

There was a knock on the door. "Jody, I have to go. Someone's at my door."

"Come in."

It was the person from the lab, Darlene. She had a file in her hand and gave it to him.

"Is this the file we were looking for?"

"I believe so. The markings on the casting match these exactly. So, it's the same shooter. Nobody else would mark their bullets with someone else's mark. Besides that, how would they know the marks?" Darlene spoke softly and placed her hands on her hips.

"Was this a guy for hire? Nobody would steal the markings from another individual or he'd end up dead!"

"What was the case and who was the Agent working the case?" Director asked.

"Sir, there was a man leaving the bank downtown and was shot by a man in a black car. The man didn't die. The man, Mr. Franklin didn't see who it was and only remembered falling to the sidewalk and the ambulance picking him up."

"The castings at the scene are precisely the same as these casting. Agent Haines was the Agent in charge of the case."

"Was a suspect picked up?"

"Yes, but because they couldn't find the weapon or the bullets, the case was dismissed."

"How long ago?"

"It was about three years ago."

"There have been no other shootings of this type until now."

"Is there any mention of a partner of Agent Haines?"

"Yes, sir, Agent Marks. He was transferred to California."

"Did we transfer him, or did he request to transfer himself?"

"I don't know, sir. That isn't my department. You'll have to check personnel."

"Thank you, Darlene. Please keep this to yourself. If anyone asks you anything about what you were looking for or what it was you found, keep it to yourself."

"Yes, sir."

Picking up his phone, and call Chief Johnson. He had promised to call him for Jolene. Finding it strange also, there was no answer. It rang several times and still no answer. He called the police department and asked for him. There told him he had called in and said he was going fishing. He'd be back in a few days.

"Did he mention what lake he was going to?"

"No sir, he didn't. I know he goes ice fishing on Lake Cancan. It seemed a little odd, for the lake isn't frozen this time of year out this time of the year."

"Thank you."

Now he was worried, too. Nobody went ice fishing this time of the year! He couldn't tell Jolene or she'd knock out the Agent protecting her and find her father.

The Director called down to get one agent to out to the lake and see if they could find Chief Johnson. It concerned him he didn't have his cell phone with him. He'd know Jolene would call him and, as everyone knew, he wouldn't have gone ice fishing this time of the year. Something had to wrong.

Agent Hanks came to his office and was surprised to have been called by the director. He knocked on the door and waited for the director to say come in.

"Agent Hanks, I have a special job for you to handle."

"Yes, sir."

"I need you to go out to the lake and look for Chief Johnson. He has gone up there to fish. I need you to find him and call me once you do, understand?"

"Yes, sir. Do you want me to bring him in?"

"No, just call me once you find him. Put him on your phone. Whatever you are working on, please put it aside for now, understand?"

"Yes, sir."

He took off to the lake. There was a dirt road that went around the lake, so he slowly drove around the lake until he saw signs of someone being there. He called out to see if he answered.

"Chief Johnson, this is Agent Hanks from the FBI. Please answer me if you can hear me."

Chief Johnson stood up and answered him. "Yes, I hear you."

"Chief Johnson, how can we help? Your daughter tried to call you this morning, and you didn't answer your phone. Is something wrong?"

"I just went fishing today. Tell my daughter I need some peace for a couple of days, so I went fishing. The office shouldn't have told you where I was."

"I guess they were worried about you as well."

"Is there anything we can do?"

"Go back to my office and tell them not to tell anybody where I've gone. When my daughter calls the director, tell her I'm fine. I just forgot my cell phone and I'm alright."

"There must be something wrong, sir?"

"I have to call the director. He wants to talk to you, sir."

"Okay, get him on the phone."

The phone only rang once, and the director picked it up.

"Chief Johnson, are you alright?"

"Yes sir, I just left my cell phone at home. I wanted some peace. There isn't anything wrong. Sorry to make everyone worried."

"You know how your daughter is. She would naturally panic when you didn't answer. The police station telling everyone you've gone ice fishing isn't the best cover for you either."

"Yes, everyone knows there isn't any ice this time of year."

"Please, let us know if something or someone is bother is bothering you."

"Yes sir, and I'll let your daughter know you're alright."

"If you let the office know not to tell anyone else I've gone ice fishing at the lake, I'd appreciate it. Thanks director."

"Yes sir, I will."

The director called one agent on duty, protecting Jolene. "Let me speak to our witness."

"Hello Jody, this is the Director of the FBI. We just spoke to the party you requested information on. He is fishing and is alright. Just wanted you to know."

"Thank you, Director."

He called the Police Station where Chief Johnson worked and talked to the lead police sergeant on duty. "Look, this is the Director of the FBI. I just spoke to Chief Johnson, and he had a message for all of you. He doesn't want anyone to know where he is or where he has gone. You are to tell all of your policemen not to tell anyone that is asking. Understand, this is his message to all of you."

"Yes sir. There have been a couple of calls for him already. They didn't tell us their name. They just said they would call back later."

"If they call again, try to get their name and text it to me, understand?"

"Yes, sir."

The Director knew better than tell Jolene about the calls or she wouldn't listen to anything he had to say or anyone else. Her father was more important than anything else to her in this world. So he knew he had to be very diligent in handling this.

The phone started ringing and he pulled it out of his breast pocket. It was Jolene. He knew that before he even looked at the caller ID.

"Yes Jolene, I just talked to him and he's just fine."

"Then why didn't he answer his cell phone?" Jolene asked.

"Jolene, he's being very careful. He left his cell phone at home. He didn't want anyone calling and tracing the call back to where you are. He's very smart you know." The Director state.

"Yes, I know. How do you think I learned everything I know." Jolene stated smartly.

"Okay, now we know he's okay. He isn't going to be able to be in touch for a could of days. We'll make sure he stays that way. I'm going to send a couple of guys up there where he's at dressed as fisher man so nobody will suspect anything."

"Great, that will make me feel better."

"Jolene, you have to stop worrying so much. Did you start going through those diaries yet?"

"No sir, but I'll start them today."

CHAPTER 19

"Good, that will keep your mind off everything for now."

"Yes sir."

Jolene laid out the diaries and decided to take the brides diary last. Something told her to take the brides maid diary first.

Something was drawing her attention to Judy Meda first. Jolene didn't know what it was, but she read it first. It appeared she was running the entire show. They would be married, from designing the wedding dress to the flower arrangements and church. This is strange to Jolene.

The more she read, the more confused she became. After reading about half of the diary, the more convinced there was more going on than Sharon knew about. Jolene marked the page she was on, picked up Anne Fletcher's diary, and began reading it.

It appeared she didn't like the way Judy was running the show. But because it was her friend, Sharon said nothing. She kept her mouth shut until Sharon said something. Besides, Judy had great taste in scents, and her decorating skills were better than Sharon's.

Ann knew July had gone with the groom a couple of years ago. She hadn't told Sharon, and until Judy told her, she wouldn't tell her either. It wasn't her place to tell her how badly he had treated her. Maybe he had changed and wasn't the person he had been back then.

Jolene saw a pattern here. It appeared he was a woman beater. There wasn't anything in Ann's diary about him ever going with her, only the fact she had picked up the pieces every time he had hit Judy.

Jolene picked Judy's diary again and when to the page she had stopped at. It appeared there were four best men. The origin of the fourth best man was a mystery to her. She needed to talk to Harold Tomas. She knew the Director wouldn't approve of that.

Jolene was going to have to get the director or another agent to call him and see what he had to say. This would not be easy for the question she had to ask. They would know what to ask or why they had to ask them.

Jolene wanted to get back out there on this case. It didn't matter to her if they were after her. She could protect herself in her eyes!

Picking up the phone, she dialed the Director cell. It rang twice, and he picked it up.

"Look Director, bring me in. I have to question a couple of people in this case. I'm convinced it has everything to do with this case we were working on. I have to question them. Bring me in and I can explain everything."

"Jolene, I can't trust you questioning anyone with this case you and agent Haines were working on. I still believe it was this case, and they were after you!"

"But sir, if it was this case, we were working on, then why haven't there been any threats against me?"

"I don't know Jolene, but you have to trust me. Agent Blay is being discharged today. And I'm bringing him to the office. I can bring you in to meet up with him. But you can't question anyone about this case. Understand Jolene?"

"Yes sir, but can I bring him up to speed where we are today?" Jolene was very persistence in her request.

"Jolene I rather you didn't, for that will make him want to follow up with you on what you have found."

"Okay, I understand. Just bring me in and I promise to behave myself."

"You better behave or I'll take you off this case." The director told her.

"Get dressed, and I'll have them bring you in. They'll bring you in by the back entrance."

Jolene was excited, for she was going to see Elliot Blay. It had been over a week since he was shot. She still didn't know how Agent Haines was getting along. The Director kept avoiding the question. Agent Blay didn't have any communication with him, either. When he'd asked the nurses, they would just say he was progressing.

It had been dark when they had taken Jolene from the Director's office. Now it was daylight, and it was taking forever to get to the office. She noticed there was nothing but woods around where they had taken her. This was a perfect place for an ambush, she thought to herself. Why would he have taken her so far out of town? The question ran through her mind. He must have had a good reason.

It had been almost forty minutes, and finally she saw the building coming into view. The FBI building was soon in view. The agents pulled up to the back entrance. Before they stopped, they surveyed their surroundings. They got out of the car and walked around to the back door and one agent opened the door while the other kept his back toward her and had his pistol drawn out of its holster. They escorted her up to the director's office.

He opened the door and told her to come in. The two agents he dismissed and told them to wait downstairs until he called them. Jolene looked around looking for Agent Blay. To her surprise, he wasn't there.

"Jolene, don't panic, he's on his way."

"I wasn't panicking. I was just surprised he was here yet. You had me way out o town and he is just a few blocks away. That's all, sir."

"Well, we have to be careful, so we had to drive him around a few blocks before bringing him in. We still don't know what case this was supposed to be about."

"Does he know how Agent Haines is coming along?"

"Jolene, we have kept his condition under the black cloud. Nobody knows how his condition is. We've just told everyone he's progressing."

"That's not fair! Doesn't Agent Blay even know? He was in the same hospital with him."

"No, we've kept everyone from knowing about his condition."

"Okay, sir. That newspaper reporter still noising around?" Jolene had a smirk on her face.

"Yes, he has me seeing a prostitute on the side and my wife somehow now believes it. This is the second or third time you have come up the back stairs and he has been hiding in the shadows somehow. He's been hiding down there in the garage and has reported it. The paper is full of it!"

"Can't you explain to her or him it's just me you are hiding out?"

"That would be the easy way out of this mess. No, I can't let whoever it is her know we are hiding you. If they got wind of that, it just wouldn't be good. So, my wife just made a big scene and left with a suitcase in hand. She is going to stay with her sister for a few days. Once this whole thing is over, she'll come back and we'll explain everything to her."

There was a knock on his office door. He knew it had to be Agent Blay. "Jolene, get in the other room. I believe it's Agent Blay, but just in case it isn't, I want to be sure."

She did as she was told and moved to the other room. She heard the door open and the director speak. "Hello Agent Blay. How are you feeling?"

"Fine, sir."

"Agent Blay, can you tell me anything you remember about the shooting?"

"No sir, it happened so fast. We had barely enough time to react. I remember a black car racing through the garage at a high rate of speed and bullets flying everywhere. Agent Haines was to the left of me and I saw him fall to the pavement. I tried to get to him, but I was shot as well."

"Did you see the driver of the car, and was there anyone with him in the car?"

"Sir, I remember seeing only one person in the car. There could have been more than one person, but I don't remember. I remember wondering if Agent Johnson had made it to safety. She had gone back inside the building for something she forgot."

The director pushed the button on his desk to the other room and told Jolene to come out from the other room.

She knew it was going to be hard for her to keep her composure when she saw him, but that was what the director expected.

"Hello Agent Blay. I'm glad you are alright. I'm glad to see you are out of the hospital. We have been worried about you and Agent Haines."

"Agent Haines is doing alright. You know, Agent Blay, you are going to have to be put into protective custody until we find out what this is all about. We still don't know if this was tied to this case you were working on with Jolene or something Agent Haines worked on before. We suspect this is about something he worked several months ago before you two came into the picture. But never the less we have to take extra precautions."

"What does that mean, sir?"

"Well, let me tell him."

"He's going to make you go out into the woods and hide for a time. Nobody will know where you are, or how to get hold of you. You'll have one of his trick phones that only lets you call him and you can't talk but a couple of minutes. Did I leave out anything, sir?"

"Come on Jolene, it hasn't been that bad."

"Then can he be sentenced with me in my hiding place? I could use the help to go over those diaries."

"I guess I could send you two together if you promise to get this job done! No hanky -pancy to go on, do you understand?"

"Yes sir, we promise!" They both said at the same time.

He knew this was just a ploy to get him not to separate them. The director wants to get down to the bottom of this case and knew with the two of them working together; he stood a better chance of getting the answers he was looking for. He also knew Jolene won't let this case go, so if they were working together, he would get this case solved.

His phone was ringing, and he knew he had to answer it. It was his secretary, and she told him it was the hospital calling about Agent Haines. He dreaded the call. It had to be bad news he freed.

"Hello, this is Director Brooks. How can I help you?"

"Director, there is someone here that would like to speak to you."

He waited a minute, and there was no one on the other end. He thought this was going to be some kind of trick. Then he heard the voice. Although raspy, he recognized it was Agent Haines.

"Oh, my goodness! Are you alright?" He asked.

"Yes sir. Where is my partner?"

"He's right here, standing beside of me. Do you want to talk to him?"

"Yes, and I want to talk to Jolene too."

"Great, I'll tell you a story. This had nothing to do with the case we're working right now. Director, do you remember the Rodrigues case? It was a gang outfit that had claimed the territory of downtown, and we went in and cleaned it up. I think we put most of their gang in prison. They swore to get even. This was their way of telling us they were back."

"Okay, so in this case, you guys were working now had nothing to do with it." The director gave a sigh of relief.

"I'm sure if they did a good job with the forensic team, they found blood there that wasn't ours."

"Your right and we couldn't get a match to anyone." The Director stated.

"I knew I got a shot off and thought I hit him, but I wasn't sure. The car was just like the one back when we had another case. I'm sure the casing was marked with a special marking."

"Yes, you're right again."

"We've placed Jolene in protective custody, and it is making her crazy. Now that Agent Blay is out of the hospital, we are placing him in protective custody as well. Now that we know which case this was tied to, there isn't any reason to do so."

"No, sir, they can go back to work. The doctors tell me I will be discharged in a few more days. Hopefully, they'll have this case solved by the time I get out."

"You wish, old man!" Jolene spoke out.

"Come on Jolene, you know I love you!" Agent Haines stated.

"Hey you two, I'm your boss and I'm standing right here!" The director stated.

"So, since this is all cleared up, can we go back to our normal conditions?" Agent Blay asked.

"I don't see why not! In fact, is would be a great idea for all of you to get back to your jobs. Maybe I can get my wife back." The director said and then laughed.

"Get your wife back?" Agent Blay asked.

"It's a long story. I'll fill you in later." Jolene said.

"Director, what about my father? Can you get a hold of the Agent out there with him and tell him it's safe to come home?" Jolene asked.

"Yes, I'll call him and tell him the coast is clear."

"Sleeping in my bed tonight will make me happy. The beds I've been sleeping in have been like sleeping on a rocky road with mostly rocks."

"Come on Jolene! You know we have a budget around here and have to keep with in that budget! Just because you are treated like royalty around your two partners doesn't mean I have to treat you the same way."

"Come on Jolene, don't be so hard on the boss. You know he loves you too," Agent Blay stated.

"Okay, I'll take I easy on him this time." Jolene stated with a smirk on her face. "Look Chief, we need to go so I can bring Agent Blay up to speed and I need to add to my blackboard."

"Add to your black board? What the hell are you talking about?"

"Sir, you don't want to know. Jolene has this unique system that works."

"Okay, if you say so. Go on and get out of here." Director looked straight at Jolene and pointed at the doorway.

Jolene and Agent Blay slipped out the back doorway and down the steps. There was a car waiting for them. The agent looked at Jolene and asked her where was they were going. He thought they were going back to the house in the woods.

The weather was really nasty, and it looked like there was another thunderstorm coming up. The sky was turning black, and the thunder was loud, along with the flashes of lightning. It seems to flash every five seconds. She knew it wasn't, but in her mind, it appeared to be. Her father was always around when a thunderstorm appeared. She hoped he was home now. She couldn't wait to see him. It had been more than two weeks since she had been home.

They pulled up in the driveway, and the agent got out of the car. He opened the back door to the car and let Jolene out. Agent Blay opened his own door and walked up to the front door waiting on Jolene. He called back to the agent driving. "Hey can you do me a favorite?"

"Sure, what can I do for you?"

"There is this pizza place down the block. Can you pick me up a large pizza? I'd order it but, the director doesn't want to many people knowing I'm out of the hospital yet."

"Sure, I'll pick you up one. What do you want on it?"

"Everything they have. Jolene, is there anything you want extra on it?" Agent Blay asked.

"No, everything on it will be good enough."

"Okay, I'll be back in a few minutes." The agent drove off toward the pizza joint.

"Agent Blay, know you have some nerve! You get out of the hospital and in just a couple of hours, you are already looking for food. You must have a tapeworm!"

"Come on Jolene, the hospital food, well it's not very good and they wouldn't let me go down to the canteen or order anything outside the hospital. Look how much weigh I've lost!"

Jolene began laughing hysterically. She couldn't believe he was saying such things. He looked the same as he did when he was admitted to the hospital. "You are so full of yourself!"

CHAPTER 20

Jolene was working on the blackboard when there was a knock on the door. She moved toward it and then stopped.

"Jolene, wait. Let me see who it is."

"Sure, but if it's your pizza, it's going to get waterlogged."

Agent Blay walked over to the door and looked through the peephole. It was his pizza.

Sleeping in my bed tonight will make me happy. The beds I've been sleeping in have been like sleeping on a rocky road with mostly rocks."

"Come on Jolene! You know we have a budget around here and have to keep with in that budget! Just because you are treated like royalty around your two partners doesn't mean I have to treat you the same way."

"Come on Jolene, don't be so hard on the boss. You know he loves you too," Agent Blay stated.

"Okay, I'll take I easy on him this time." Jolene stated with a smirk on her face. "Look Chief, we need to go so I can bring Agent Blay up to speed and I need to add to my blackboard."

"Add to your black board? What the hell are you talking about?"

"Sir, you don't want to know. Jolene has this unique system that works."

"Okay, if you say so. Go on and get out of here." Director looked straight at Jolene and pointed at the doorway.

Jolene and Agent Blay slipped out the back doorway and down the steps. There was a car waiting for them. The agent looked at

Jolene and asked her where was they were going. He thought they were going back to the house in the woods.

The weather was really nasty, and it looked like there was another thunderstorm come up. The sky was turning black, and the thunder was loud, along with the flashes of lightning. It seems to flash every five seconds. She knew it wasn't, but in her mind, it appeared to be. Her father was always around when a thunderstorm appeared. She hoped he was home now. She couldn't wait to see him. It had been more that two weeks since she had been home.

They pulled up in the driveway, and the agent got out of the car. He opened the back door to the car and let Jolene out. Agent Blay opened his own door and walked up to the front door waiting on Jolene. He called back to the agent driving. "Hey can you do me a favorite?"

"Sure, what can I do for you?"

"There is this pizza place down the block. Can you pick me up a large pizza? I'd order it but, the director doesn't want to many people knowing I'm out of the hospital yet."

"Sure, I'll pick you up one. What do you want on it?"

"Everything they have. Jolene, is there anything you want extra on it?" Agent Blay asked.

"No, everything on it will be good enough."

"Olay, I'll be back in a few minutes." The agent drove off toward the pizza joint.

"Agent Blay, know you have some nerve! You get out of the hospital and in just a couple of hours, you are already looking for food. You must have a tapeworm!"

"Come on Jolene, the hospital food, well it's not very good and they wouldn't let me go down to the canteen or order anything outside the hospital. Look how much weigh I've lost!"

Jolene began laughing hysterically. She couldn't believe he was saying such things. He looked the same as he did when he was admitted to the hospital. "You are so full of yourself!"

Jolene was working on the blackboard when there was a knock on the door. She moved toward it and then stopped.

"Jolene, wait. Let me see who it is."

"Sure, but if it's your pizza, it's going to get waterlogged."

Agent Blay walked over to the door and looked through the peephole. It was his pizza.

"Hey, how much was it? Jolene, do you have any money? Can you pay Ray? Agent Hopkins?"

"Sure, Ray how much was it?"

"Well, I hope it's good, they charged me twenty."

"Sorry about that, when we call ahead and they know it's for the Chief it's only like fifteen."

"That's okay Jolene. I don't mind feeding the animals. Is there anything else I can do you?"

"No, not now Ray. But if there is can I call you? The director doesn't want us circulating out just yet."

"Just call me. Here's my card. I'm surprised I hadn't met you yet. I saw you at the ceremony but I couldn't get close enough to meet you."

"Okay Ray, move along. Your time is up." Agent Blay was showing his disapproval of him talking to Jolene.

After he left Jolene looked at Elliot and with her hands on her hips she stood there patiently waiting for him to say something, He was too busy digging into the pizza. It was like he hadn't eaten for a year!

"Elliot, look at me! What in the world is wrong with you? I've never seen you be so disagreeable to another agent before. What is your problem?"

"Jolene, he was plainly hitting on you! Couldn't you see that? You belong to me and nobody else. I'm letting everyone know it too!"

"Elliot, if you are going to act like this every time someone comes around. I don't know if I like that or not. You know I'm not a piece of property you can take possession of. Do you understand that?"

"I'm so sorry Jolene. It's still so new to me! I've never felt like this before and I'm so scared I'll lose you. Please forgive me. Come on and eat something and then we can get down to work, okay?"

"But never do this again, understand?"

"Yes."

"Elliot, you have eaten almost half the pizza by yourself!"

"Hey, I told you I was hungry!"

There was a car pulling up in the driveway but it was too dark to see exactly what kind it was. Not to scare Jolene because it was still storming. He knocked on the door to let her know he was coming in.

"Jolene, it's dad! I'm coming in. Jolene, I know you're here."

Jolene took off running toward the door. "Oh dad, I'm so glad to see you."

"Not as glad as I am to see you. Jolene, I know this is your job now. But do you realize I almost had a heart attack?"

"I knew if anybody knew what ice fishing meant you would, that's why I told the boys down at the store where I was going you would know right away and they would find me if you needed me."

"Yes, as soon as they told me you went Ice fishing, I knew exactly where you went."

"Boy dad, this is some storm. Did the boys from the FBI have a problem getting you out of the woods?"

"No, they knew exactly where I was and they came right to me. They told me you were at this place alongside this big oak tree and what's where we went? That was right where I was. It's a good thing too. With this rainstorm, it's a good thing."

"Remember when I was little? Rainstorms always scared me. I would always run to you. You would always chase the storm away."

"What is Elliot doing here?"

"They let him out of the hospital today. He's in my custody for now. I have to make sure he does nothing. He sudden." Jolene said proudly."

"Does that include eat a whole pizza?"

"Yeah, have some dad."

"Thanks Jolene, don't mind if I do."

CHAPTER 21

"Okay Jolene, what have you been doing? I know Agent Haines is still in the hospital and Agent Blay just was released. I'm surprised he is here with you. Is everything okay?"

"Yes dad, everything is okay. Because he was just release, the director thought is would be easier if he stayed here with us for a few days. Be sides with you here, you can help him where I can't."

"Okay, but dad if it becomes too much, please let me know and we'll make different arrangements."

"Jolene, just pretend I'm not here. Do what you normally do."

"We are going over the diaries from the bridesmaid. There had to be some type of clue in one of them. Elliot can help me read over them. He has to pick up something that I might now see."

"What have you picked up on so far?" Jolene's dad asked.

"It appears the groom went with all three bridesmaids. The only one that has anything extra to say about the wedding is this wedding should have been hers. That I can't see. But I haven't been through all the diaries yet."

"What gave you that idea?" Dad asked.

"Well, the dress the bride was going to wear was hers and the underwear, shoes and the hairstyle of the bride were from her pictures. Everything was set up to exact everything she would have done for her wedding."

"But what about the groom? Does it say anything about him?"

"Funny you should ask. The groom what the same groom, Mr. Tomas. I haven't gone through each diary yet but it's apparent each woman, the bride's maid, had gone with Mr. Tomas. The only thing I haven't figured out is there are three bridesmaids."

"Who is the third one?"

"Is it not listed in one diary?" Agent Blay asked.

"So far, I haven't found it. But here is the funny part. All the women were exactly the same size. They even wore the same size shoes, hair was the same length and color." Jolene stated.

"I think we need to talk to Mr. Tomas again and see what he to say about dating these women. He must remember dating each one of them, don't you think?"

"You know, if I think about it, I think I can remember every girl I dated when I was in high school. How about you, sir?"

"No, I'm afraid when I met Jolenes mother, all my memories disappeared."

"Oh, dad you are so sweet. Maybe that's why we're so close. It appears the storm is letting up. I don't hear as much thunder as before."

"I believe you two need to get a hold of Mr. Tomas and see about any other women in his life. He certainly doesn't seem that upset about his bride's death or her maid of honors. He has to know something more. Why is he nosing around with everything else?"

"He isn't upset about losing his bride to be?" Sheriff Johnson asked.

"That's just it, dad. He's more about running rumors in the paper about everyone else. Including the Director of the FBI."

"I'm not sure Dad, but he had the Director seeing a prostate and his wife left him because of it." Jolene was anger about it.

"But you knew better, right?"

"Dad, it was me, dressed up like a prostate. I would leave by the back stairway and left in a car with the windows blacked out."

"Oh, I see." Chief Johnson laughed.

"Yes, and his wife was in on it. But you see what I was talking about. If something happened to Elliot or me, I would be heartbroken. Not traveling around looking for rumors about other people."

"Jolene, I think you should see this Mr. Tomas tomorrow. The weather is supposed to be clear and you know where he works, right?"

"Yes, and then you can baby sit Elliot." Jolene said.

"Oh yeah? Why do I get the job of baby-sitting? Because I can't take him with me. I can't leave him alone here with the board. He will mess it up and it'll take me forever to straighten it out."

"Okay, I see what you mean."

The day looked like it was going to be a real nice day. The sun was shining and the birds were singing. Jolene was sitting at the table eating a bowl of cereal. She saw the bird feeder was full of water. She had to take care of it. Walking out to it she poured the water out and dried up the water. Pouring new food in the feeder it didn't take long for the birds to flock back to it.

Jolene looked over her notes on Mr. Tomas and while she took a shower went over the question, she wanted to ask him. She hoped he would trip himself up with a wrong answer.

Sheriff Johnson was going to his office. The deputies would be glad to see him. He had been gone for over two weeks. This was very unusual for him to be out of the office this long. Now he had to figure out what to do with Agent Blay. He knew he couldn't leave him there alone. Jolene had already warned him.

"Agent Blay, let's shine on you're going to work with me today!"

"What do you mean, going to work with you today?" Blay was totally in the dark.

"Well, it's like this. Jolene doesn't want you here by yourself. So sice I'm in charge, you are going with me to the station house and see how a real police department is run,"

"Oh, she didn't. She made you, my babysitter?"

"Yes, she did. She told me you couldn't be trusted around that blackboard and, frankly, I agree with her."

"Look, I can promise you I won't go near it. I'll go over the dairies and behave myself."

"No, my daughter would never forgive me if I let you stay here. I'm with her. I know you too well, and I believe in my daughter. If she says you'll do something, then you do it."

"I can't go to the police station with you. They will all laugh at me. Don't you understand?"

"Look, we'll tell them you just got out of the hospital and they didn't want you to be alone for a few days, so I told them I'd look after you for a while. How does that sound? We don't have to stay all day, just for a couple of hours, so I can see what's going on in my station. You know I was gone for a few days myself."

"Yes sir, I know. I guess as long as they think I'm still recovering, we can get by with it."

Jolene drove up to the newspaper office and hoped Mr. Tomas was working. He hadn't missed one day of work. He was registered to take off one day for his honeymoon after he was married. This made little sense.

"Hello Mr. Tomas. I'm with the FBI. I'm sure you remember me. I questioned you after your bride to be disappeared."

"Oh yes, you had two other FBI agents with you. What can I do for you, Agent Johnson, I believe?"

"What can you tell me about your bride to be?"

"I do not know as what you are talking about."

"It appears you went with all three women, and then you chose Sharon to marry. How did you arrive at that decision?"

"I guess she was the lucky one. There were others, you know."

"What do you mean, there were others? Was this some kind of contest?"

"I guess you could say it was a contest of sorts. They had to have the right measurements, hair color, measurements, and do my bidding from top to bottom."

"You have to be some sort of sick fool to believe a woman would do everything you asked and want nothing for herself." Jolene was becoming angry the more she spoke to him.

"No, these were the best out of the lot and Sharon was the closest to doing everything I asked. I knew I could change her in any way I wanted with a little training Id have the perfect wife. One that all men would die for." Mr. Tomas stated smugly.

"There was only one more question I have for you?"

"Yes, go ahead."

"Don't you have to feel some expression of love for the person you are going to marry?"

"FBI Johnson, love has nothing to do with it. Maybe you can answer a question for me?"

"Go ahead."

"Everything had been arranged for our wedding, with one exception. At the last minute, Judy said we needed one more groomsman, for there was one more bridesmaid she wasn't aware of until they left for the real Jolene drove up to the newspaper office and hoped Mr. Tomas was working. He hadn't missed one day of work. He was registered to take off one day for his honeymoon after he was married. This made little sense.

"Hello Mr. Tomas. I'm with the FBI. I'm sure you remember me. I questioned you after your ride to be disappeared."

"Oh yes, you had two other FBI agents with you. What can I do for you, Agent Johnson, I believe?"

"What can you tell me about your bride to be?"

"I do not know as what you are talking about."

"It appears you went with all three women, and then you chose Sharon to marry. How did you arrive at that decision?"

"I guess she was the lucky one. There were others, you know."

"What do you mean, there were others? Was this some kind of contest?"

"I guess you could say it was a contest of sorts. They had to have the right measurements, hair color, measurements, and do my bidding from top to bottom."

"You have to be some sort of sick fool to believe a woman would do everything you asked and want nothing for herself." Jolene was becoming angry the more she spoke to him.

"No, these were the best out of the lot and Sharon was the closest to doing everything I asked. I knew I could change her in any way I wanted with a little training Id have the perfect wife. One that all men would die for." Mr. Tomas stated smugly.

"There was only one more question I have for you?"

"Yes, go ahead."

"Don't you have to feel some expression of love for the person you are going to marry?"

"FBI Johnson, love has nothing to do with it. Maybe you can answer a question for me?"

"Go ahead."

"Everything had been arranged for our wedding, with one exception. At the last minute, Judy said we needed one more groomsman, for there was one more bridesmaid she wasn't aware of until they left for the real estate seminar. Judy and I had worked out everything down to the last minute."

"Do you have this person's name?"

"No, I don't. The measurements of the groomsman had to be very specific, and I would have to get the tailor to do up the tux for him."

"So, you didn't have a gentleman picked out just encase someone couldn't attend?" Jolene smirked back at him.

"Look, this was thrown at me at the last minute. Judy didn't tell me who it was or where he came from. I was told this was needed. I tried to get it done. This was the only thing Judy asked of me. I'm not sure Judy had approved of it, for she was waiting for the last minute to tell me about it."

"So, if you said it couldn't be done, then Judy would have told Sharon it couldn't be done and that would have been the end, right?"

"Yes, that would have been the end, but I could get a hold of the tailor and he could do it. Everything was set."

"Thank you, Mr. Tomas. That will be all for now." Jolene shook his hand and then turned to walked out of his office.

All of a sudden Jolene turned and faced Mr. Tomas. "Mr. Tomas, what if something happened to Sharon? Would you look for another bride?"

"That's an easy question. Judy is next in line, and then Ann. They all have the availability to become Mrs. Tomas."

"Thank you again Mr. Tomas." Jolene turned and walked out.

CHAPTER 22

Agent Blay and Jolene were still going over the diaries of three women. Agent Blay jumped up from the table and looked at Jolene. His mouth was open, but no words were coming out. Jolene looked at him, wondering if she should call someone. She couldn't figure out what was going on with him.

"Elliot, are you okay? Answer me?" Jolene panicked!

"Jolene, I can't believe what I just read."

"Well, tell me?"

"Judy, who was one of the brides maid, had everything planned out so everything would be her perfect wedding! The Chapel, wedding dress, flowers, food for the reception all the guests who were invited down to the minister to perform the ceremony!"

"We know she was to set up the plans for the wedding. But what you are telling me she had planned this wedding around her wedding?" Jolene replied.

"Yeah, that's what her diary says! I wonder if any of them read this before we did?" Elliot asked.

"I wouldn't think so. For if Sharon read this, she would have cast her out of the wedding before it happened." Jolene said and rolled her eyes.

"Hey, Chief Johnson, what are you cooking? It sure smells good. You know the way to my heart!"

"That's dad's famous chili. I told him how much you love chili, so he said he'd make a big pot just for you!"

"Oh, you little smart ass! Did you tell him I almost died?" Agent Blay came back at Jolene.

"Sheriff Johnson, Jolene said you were making chili?"

"Yes, Jolene told me you like chili and she told me what happened to you with chili at that little cafe. I promise this is mild just for you."

Jolene was laughing. "Yes, I told him. He said he was going to make it mild."

"Okay, back to work." Jolene ordered.

"Come on Jolene. We've been at it since early this morning. We have to take a break. Besides that, my arm is hurting, so let's take a thirty-minute break. Chief Johnson, what do you think?"

"Jolene, yes, you guys should take a break. You know if you keep pushing your bond to miss something. Take a few minutes to walk around, go outside, walk down the block."

She knew he was right. "Okay, we'll go for a walk around the block." Jolene wasn't too happy about the decision they had made and it was about to rain.

"Jolene, take a light jacket with you. It looks like it's going to rain. The wind might be blowing a little."

"Elliot, what do you think Judy was planning to do with Sharon to get her out of the way?" Jolene asked Elliot.

"I don't know or understand why she would have put something like that in her diary unless she planned to bump her off."

"I understand that, but they were best friends. At least, that is what Mr. Tomas stated. But he also said she would be the next in line to marry him if something happened to Sharon."

"Was he serious when he said that?"

"Most definitely. There was no joking around on his part. He said if something happened to the two of them. Ann would be the third choice. No hesitation in his voice at all. It was as he was playing a game or something."

"Look Elliot let's head back to the house. I don't want to get caught out here if it starts to rain." Every time the thunder sounded Jolene would jump.

"Jolene, it's just a little thunder. Why are you so scare?"

"I don't know, I just am."

They turned around and headed back to the house. Jolene's father was standing at the doorway waiting. He knew Jolene was terrified of thunder storms.

Tomorrow is supposed to be better. No clouds and no thunder storms. "Jolene You'll love the weather tomorrow." Chief Johnson stated.

"Chief, you promise?" Jolene asked.

"Yes, I listened to the weather and that's what the said."

"Great, I want to go back to see Joe. Do you remember him, Elliot?"

"Wasn't he the guy sitting on the bench in the park?"

"Yes, I want to see him again. I have a feeling about him. I think he saw more than he's telling us. I believe the police have turned him away so many times, he just keeps everything to himself."

"Wasn't he in Malta? I bet he's till sitting on that bench in the park."

"When do we head there?" Elliot asked.

"Let's plan ongoing in the morning. I's supposed to be clear, and the sun is supposed to be shining." Jolene said with a positive attitude.

"Okay, you're really upset by thunderstorms, aren't you?" Elliot spoke slowly.

"Yes, ever since she was a little girl, they have always bothered her. Nobody knows why." Chief Johnson spoke up,

"Is the chili ready, dad?"

"Yes, come and get it."

Agent Blay was the first one through the kitchen door. He was starving. He didn't want them to know, but he really wanted something to eat.

At first, he just sipped the chili to test how hot it was. The spice he tasted wasn't that bad. This was the first time he didn't have to be afraid of eating something that would take the skin off his mouth.

"See, Dad has just the right amount of spice to keep it interesting without making it deadly!"

"Yes, it's fantastic!" Elliot told him.

"So Jolene, have you decided what your next move is going to be?"

"Yes, you said the forecast for tomorrow was going to be clear. So we're going to Malta and see this witness I talked to a few days ago. He saw this car pull up to the park and dump the body, or that's what he said. I want to talk to him again. I believe he knows more than he's saying."

"What do you think, Elliot? Does he appear to know more?"

"Sir, I really don't know, for he only would talk to Jolene alone. Agent Haines and myself weren't invited."

"That sounds a little suspicious to me. Jolene I know you know what you're doing, but be extra careful, you hear me?"

"Yes dad, I will. There was something about him, I don't know exactly what it was, but I have to see for myself what it was I saw or heard in his voice."

"How do you propose to find him again?" Chief asked.

"He told me where he lived and he told us he was always in the park seating on the park bench during the day."

"Okay, just be real, careful."

"Yes Dad, Elliot and I will."

CHAPTER 23

Chief Johnson took Agent Blay home. Chief wanted a couple of minutes alone with him to discuss his dealings with his daughter. He knew he was very fond of her and she was fond of him. He didn't know exactly how much their love for each other had gone.

"Look, I'll pick you up in the morning when I go to work so Jolene doesn't have to drive over here. Is that okay?"

"Okay with me. I don't know what Jolene has in mind, but she must know something I don't." Agent Bay stated.

"Well, you know, you have worked with her to know she works on a different plane than the rest of us," Chief stressed.

"Yes, I know. Every time I think I've figured her out, she pulls a miracle out of the hat and we all look in amazement. Even Agent Haines sees the same thing. He told me just go with it and don't figure it out.'"

"That was good advice." Chief stated.

Next morning chief picked Agent Blay up at seven and drove him back to his house. Jolene was ready to go and had her briefcase loaded and ready to rock and roll.

"Thanks dad, I would have picked him up. This saves us time. Ready to ride Elliot?" Jolene asked.

"Sure, I am Jolene." They walked out to the car together. Chief Johnson got in his car and went to work.

It was a thirty-minute drive to Malta and with Jolene driving, well, it was thirty minutes. With Agent Haines driving, it was nearly forty-five minutes.

Jolene droves slowly around the park and looked out to see if she could see Joe sitting on a bench.

"Look Elliot, there he is."

"Jolene, there is a parking place right in front of hm. You don't think it'll scare him if you park there do you?"

"I don't believe so."

Jolene pulled into the space and watched Joe. He didn't move, just sat still and watched Jolene to see what she did next.

She got out of the car and moved toward him slowly. She didn't want to scare him off. He already knew who she was and that she was with the FBI.

As she drew closer, he stood up. Jolene wasn't sure what he was going to do. "Joe, this is Jolene. Remember meeting me a couple of weeks ago?"

"Yes, pretty lady, come and set down with me."

"Okay Joe. I want to ask you some question if that's alright?"

"Sure."

"Joe, it's about those girls that were killed. Did you speak to any of them?"

"Yes, the one girl named Ann. She stopped by here looking for a Chinese restaurant we have here in town."

"Did you give her direction to find it?"

"Well, kind of."

"What do you mean, kind of?"

"Well, I told her I'd take her to it. I took her to the front door. She promised to buy me a meal. She kept her promise and bought me a complete Chinese meal."

"Okay, did she drive you back to the park?"

"Yes, she drove me back to my place over there. We walked inside and she sat with me while I ate."

"Did she tell you about her friends?"

"Yes, she told me because it was getting late, they would look for her. Sure enough, another one named Judy came by the park looking for her. She saw her car parked at the parked."

"What did you do about the second girl?"

"I had some chloroform, and I knocked out Ann and then walked over to the park and met Judy."

"Did you tell her where Ann was?"

"Not at first. I told her Ann was having car trouble and told her I'd look at it as soon as the motor cooled down."

"We came up in one car. I borrowed this car to look for her. There are three of us here together. We're all in real estate. I guess I should call Sharon and tell her what happened to us. I know she is going to be worried."

"Who did you borrow this car from?" Joe had asked.

"A guy at the hotel. He had gone to the seminar with us. I'll tell Sharon what happened and to tell Nick what happened and I'll bring the car back as soon as our car is fixed."

"Okay."

They walked across the street to his apartment. As soon as she opened the door, she saw Ann laying on a cot. She ran over to her. Joe put the cloth over her face and knocked her out.

Now all I had to do was wait on the third one to show up. What they didn't realize Joe wasn't that old. He was only like sixty years old and had been a surgeon. He had been kicked out of the medical profession for illegally performing surgeries on women.

"Joe, that's why you give the police such a hard time, isn't it?"

"Yes, I'm looking for them to arrest me and put me away. But they only think I'm doing all these things to draw attention to myself. I've told them I killed these women. They just laughed at me!"

"Joe, how did you get the car back to the hotel?"

"I drove it back to the hotel and the girls' car I put down in the lake."

Jolene looked over at the car and motioned for Agent Blay to come over.

"Agent Blay, please put the cuffs on Joe. Read him his rights. Is there anything you need us to do with your apartment?"

"All the evidence you need is still there. I preserved it for you."

"Agent Blay, I'll call the forensic team and get them out here."

"Jolene, what do we do with this guy?"

"We'll take him to my father's jail until we can transport him to federal lockup. Thank you, Joe, for being so honest with me." Jolene told him and placed her hand on his shoulder.

"You are such a pretty lady. I know you are still looking for an answer to one more question. Why did I remove their breast?"

"Yes, I would like to know."

"A physician did that to my mother when he told her she had cancer and to keep it from spreading, he needed to remove both her breast. It was a lie. So, I practiced until I could do it better than he ever thought it could be done. I know it wasn't right. But they felt no pain, not like my mother."

"That's why you kept bugging the police to lock you up. So, you won't go on killing. But they were no help. They thought you were a nuisance. Even when you told them what you saw that night with one body being dumped in the park. Is that right Joe?"

"Yes, pretty lady. I knew you would be back to see me. You believed me when I talked and I could see it in your eyes you would be back to see me. Thank you, pretty lady and thank you for believing in me."

The End.